PRAISE FOR

MORE THAN ONE VOICE

"...be swept up in the imagination and creativity of these incredible young people."

—Marlin M. Jenkins

"...he noticed the door was creaked open. The boy yelled in a curious way, "Anybody there?" As he expected, nobody answered."

—Levi Athias

"The shard isn't an ordinary slice of glass. It has these strange markings on it, almost like it was from hundreds of years ago."

—Natasha Dutton

MORE THAN ONE VOICE

SHORT FICTION BY 6TH GRADERS

A PUBLICATION BY 826 MSP

ISBN 13: 978-1-63489-637-5

Library of Congress Catalog Number has been applied for.
Printed in the United States of America
First Printing: 2023
27   26   25   24   23   5   4   3   2   1

Cover illustration by Daisy Illustrations (www.daisyillustrations.com)
Cover and Interior design by Vivian Steckline

wiseink.com

To order, visit itascabooks.com or call 1-800-901-3480. Reseller discounts available.

"Imagination will often carry us to worlds that never were. But without it we go nowhere."

-Carl Sagan, *Cosmos*

CONTENTS

FABLES AND ANIMAL STORIES

Mystery and Suspense Stories

Mystery and Suspense Stories

EDUCATOR RESOURCES

ACKNOWLEDGEMENTS

FOREWORD

● ● ● ● ● ● ● ● ● ● ● ● ● ● ● ●

Working with young people often reminds me of myself at those ages. It's a strange time machine to what feels like a different life. Despite "poet" or "writer" being some of the first words I'd use to describe myself now, I didn't start writing because I loved it, but because I felt like I had lost my love of reading.

I read a lot when I was in elementary school, but by middle school the spark had fizzled. So I began to write stories: it gave me something to do in my down time because I wasn't very social, it allowed me to spend more time with the video game and TV characters I loved by creating my own versions of their stories, and, most importantly, it gave me things to read that were about things I was interested in.

Soon, instead of just fanfiction, I was writing original stories with characters and worlds I had created. I fell in love with the sense of possibility that came with writing, with how powerful your own imagination can be if you spend time with it and let it move you.

Writing grows this sense of wonder and creativity, but I believe we all already have some form of it when we're young. What's unfortunate for many people is that it's easy to lose. When I taught creative writing to college students at University of Michigan, it felt like much of my job was to

help them remember how to tap into their innate creativity, to get out of their own way and see beyond just the reality around them.

Now, as a high school teacher, I have a quote from writer bell hooks permanently written on my board: "The function of art is to do more than tell it like it is—it's to imagine what is possible."

I hope as you read these pages that you'll allow yourself to be swept up in the imagination and creativity of these incredible young people. Through fables, suspense, and science fiction, these students have created worlds for us to love, turning Sandburg Middle School—and the pencils, paper, and keyboards therein—into portals to anywhere they've decided is worth visiting.

Maybe these stories will remind you of your younger self, or of how writing and reading can be both enriching and fun. Or maybe you're one of the students in these pages, proud to see your name and words immortalized in print. No matter who you are, a book like this makes it possible for us all to connect—students, teachers, volunteers, parents, readers—and be transported, together, to wherever we could possibly imagine.

In solidarity with love,
Marlin M. Jenkins

FABLES AND ANIMAL STORIES

....

THE DOVE AND THE RIVER

•　•　•　•　•　•　•　•　•　•　•　•　•　•

MARKIYA ABRAMS

T he simple, elegant Dove always flies above the River, admiring its beauty from afar. One day, as the Dove is admiring the River's grace, she spots an odd strange plant growing beside the River that she had never seen before.

The Dove in confusion flies over to the River and asks, "My beautiful graceful River, why have you sprouted a new plant?"

The River looks at the Dove with soft eyes and says, "Many people take without giving back to me, little Dove." She sighs. "So I have sprouted a poisonous plant to keep those who are selfish and unworthy of my clean waters away."

The Dove looks at the River in shock. "But why must you do that? Those animals need your water to live their lives to the fullest extent. I understand they may not give back to you, but they cannot survive without your water!" The Dove sighs at the River and flies away to devise a plan to get rid of those plants.

She looks for Mr. Fox, because he drinks from the River every day after getting done with his hunts.

"Mr. Fox! Mr. Fox! Please, oh please, I need your help!" the Dove says.

Mr. Fox looks at the Dove and flashes a big smile at her.

7

"Yes Dove, what can I help you with?" he says as calmly as possible, so as not to frighten her.

"River has grown poisonous plants near herself, so please do not go near to drink your water just yet!" the Dove says.

But just as Mr. Fox is about to say something to the Dove, she leaves as quickly as she had come. She leaves in a hurry without an explanation, not wanting anyone to get hurt. As she flies to her nest, she thinks of a plan; if she can pull those nasty poisonous plants out, nobody will be able to be poisoned by them anymore. And though it might risk her life, her animal friends and River will be safe if she follows through with it. She arrives at where the River has grown those nasty poisonous plants and starts ripping them out with her beak.

Just when she's about to get the last one, River asks, "Why risk your life for such selfish animals, kind Dove?"

Dove looks at River after she rips the plant out. "Because I care for them, River. Some of them may be selfish and mean, or angry and short tempered, but they help our land as well. They were not created just for them to be angry or selfish. They were created for a purpose, which is why I must pull these plants out: so they can serve their full purpose for as long as possible." And just as the Dove finishes that sentence, she falls into the River with a smile.

The moral for this story is that sometimes it's okay to be a little selfish, because sometimes it's what you need that has to be prioritized.

MARKIYA ABRAMS is a sixth grader from Minneapolis. She loves a good romantic anime or K-drama—and she's watched them all! Markiya prefers Skittles over chocolate and likes to write stories where the characters have complex relationships.

CINDY AND THE BUNNIES

●●●●●●●●●●●●●●●●●

MAKENNA MARTIN

One day there were two bunnies, and they were in bad conditions. This girl named Cindy was eating a snack. When she was going to throw her trash away, she saw the bunnies. So then she looked around, and she saw no one that could be their owner.

She said, "Okay, well let's see if I can do what I always wanted to do."

Cindy went to her lab room that she had in her house, then she started working on how she was going to help the bunnies. So then she thought, *What if I can give them a make-over? And I can find them a home, because they need a home.* The bunnies do not deserve to be treated badly. They need a home because if they have a home, then they are not going to get treated like that.

The next day, she was fixing up the bunnies. . . and then she thought she could give them names. She was looking at all kinds of names that she could think of. And she said Oreo and Boyd. The bunnies started jumping up and down like they were so happy that they liked the names. So then she gave them a makeover, and they were really, really pretty. Cindy was going to try to find them a home, but nobody wanted to adopt one of them. So then Cindy thought she

would have missed them if she would have found them a home. She would just keep them and adopt them both. They could not have been that happy in a long time. They were in a good home.

MAKENNA MARTIN lives with her mom and her siblings. She has a dog that likes to play a lot and sometimes she likes to get snacks and go to the grocery store for the food that she likes to eat.

REFLECTION

● ● ● ● ● ● ● ● ● ● ● ● ● ●

MUAH VANG

The glass reflects the animals like a mirror. Observing the animals carefully, I touch the reflection of myself and stare at the distance. I stare a little longer as I feel myself become transparent. The laughter and crying of children become numb in my ears. The jellyfish then wanders away and disappears like it was never there, but I still stare away at the distance quietly wondering. . . As I feel invisible, I feel nothing but the void. I feel my thoughts consume myself as I snap back to reality and continue on. But it's not the jellyfish that make me admire it, it's the aquarium that shows me its ways. I look back and the jellyfish then blends into life.

MUAH VANG previously attended Sandburg Middle School.

DON'T BULLY

● ● ● ● ● ● ● ● ● ● ● ● ● ● ● ●

JANAIS PINNEY

Once upon a time, I made six new friends and their names were Alyssa, Logan, Tommy, Julianni, Dre, and Kennedi. They were my friends but one thing that pissed me off was when Julianni bullied Kennedi because he was body shaming. We all got mad at him.

After that he got mad at us, Logan and Julianni were about to fight. Of course Logan won and everybody was happy in our small group. But one thing was that Logan was suspended for three days then came back and had one day of in-school suspension. But he and Julianni got into a fight Julianni was beaten badly. And then when he came back he had in-school suspension for four days.

JANAIS PINNEY is a sixth grade student at Sandburg Middle School. She lives in New Hope, Minn.

THE GIFT

KAREN VASQUEZ

Once upon a time, there was a girl named Lizza who lived in Canada. She liked to draw.

One day, her best friend wanted to give her a gift but she said no and then the next day, the friend passed away.

They solved the problem by Lizza receiving gifts from everyone.

That's why you should receive gifts from people because you don't know if they are giving a gift for a reason. Say yes to the gift that someone is giving.

KAREN VASQUEZ is a sixth grader at Sandburg Middle School. Her favorite way to spend time is with her parents or to go outside or play with my friends. She's got a very, very bad memory and loves animals so much.

JUDGMENT

· ● ● ● ● ● ● ● ● ● ● ● ● ● ●

ELIJAH TOWEH

D avid and his son went to Times Square, New York. They went to get clothes for school. They went to a fancy store and they saw a lot of expensive clothes like Jordans, Nike, Bape, and Chrome Hearts. The son said, "I want the Chrome Hearts hoodie and the Jordans."

There was a lady named Linda who walked by and went up to the son and David.

"Hey, I'm not trying to be rude, but these clothes are almost a thousand dollars and you guys might steal them," said Linda.

"What makes you think that?" said David.

"Well, look at you. You look broke," said Linda.

"Well, if you must know, I'm the owner of half the city and I own this store," said David, "And I can fire you."

"Hahahaha, you really think that I will buy that? Look, you better get out before I call secur–"

"Hey Mr. David, how are you?" said the boss.

"Good," said David.

"Wait, wait, wait, you guys know each other?" said Linda.

"Yeah, he's my boss and he owns half the city," said the boss.

"Miss, I think you need to fire Linda because she judged me by the way I look."

"Are you serious, Linda? You judged another customer? You know what, I can't take this anymore YOU ARE FIRED."

Elijah Toweh is a sixth grade student from Sandburg Middle School.

MUSHROOMY AND
HER PET FROG

● ● ● ● ● ● ● ● ● ● ● ● ● ● ●

LEDIA M.

Hi, I'm Mushroomy and I have a story to tell you about my pet frog. It was a beautiful day. It was morning and I woke up and went to go feed my pet frog Bubbles but when I put her food in the bowl she never came. I looked everywhere but I couldn't find her. So that's when I knew she was missing. I started to print out the lost frog photos. Then I went outside and started to hang them up. No one had called me. I waited and waited. No phone calls.

Then the next day I decided to go out and to find her. I went to her favorite place but I didn't see her. I checked her second favorite place. I thought I saw her but no, it was a different frog. I decided just to go back home but then I saw a frog.

I went up close, but someone had her on a leash. I went up to them and it was my neighbor and they said that they were headed to my house to take her to me. So they gave me my frog and went home. I got my pet frog back and she was hungry as always, so I fed her.

LEDIA M. is a sixth grade student at Sandburg Middle School. Her favorite color is neon blue and she lives

with her family. She loves to write scary stories or calming stories. She really wants to make books about her stories. She has three dogs and three cats and she loves to sleep.

DIOR BEING DIOR

• • • • • • • • • • • • • • • •

DENISE MCKISSIC

D ior is a Black girl and she is five foot three inches. She's bougie.

One day, Dior went to the pool. It was three feet to nine feet deep.

Dior started in the three foot area and made her way to six feet. Then, she went to nine feet. She could swim, but she got to the middle of nine feet and got tired of swimming.

DENISE MCKISSIC is a sixth grade student at Sandburg Middle School. She really likes animals, and has a dog, cat, and a gecko. Denise also loves spending time with her family and doing nails.

THE T-DEVIL

• ● ● ● ● ● ● ● ● ● ● ● ● ●

UZIEL CAMPOSECO ROS

The t-devil is a scavenger. They have very very sharp teeth and a good sense of smell to find carcasses. The t-devil can chew a bone in half like a chip! They can usually find other trash and recycled stuff by using their senses. They sometimes use the trash to make dens. For them, it's comfy in all that trash! For us, it would probably be uncomfy. I would rather live in a den with no trash.

T-devils can even hear a carcass fall down from a tree and it can hear other scavenger birds or other animals that are finding pieces of carcasses. They can go and fight for the food for themselves in a little pack, which is their family. Sometimes other family members come with them.

T-devils are very protective of their territories, and they're actually called Tasmanian devils. Their name comes from the Europeans, because when the Europeans were there to kill all the predators in Tasmania, they put traps everywhere to kill all the predators so that they wouldn't eat their sheep. One species went extinct at that time. It was the Tasmanian tiger. Then, when they were camping in a house and were sleeping, they heard a demonic voice howling. When they went outside to check, it was over. They went back to bed. When they heard it the second time, they found a family of Tasmanian devils howling. They called them Tasmanian devils because they sound like demons

I like them because of their sounds and their cool features like their teeth and their sense of smell. They're pretty cool because they use all of their senses to find stuff and their families if one of them gets lost.

UZIEL CAMPOSECO Ros is a sixth grade student at Sandburg Middle School.

THE BAD DAY

● ● ● ● ● ● ● ● ● ● ● ● ● ●

ANGELO WILSON

O nce upon a time, there was a family with three kids and they just kept fighting. The parents just needed a vacation so they went to a fancy hotel. They were amazed at how the hotel looked. When they went to their room they were stunned. Then, they saw their room and they had room service and they unpacked their bags and relaxed. But the kids were arguing about a toy, and the parents said, "Share!"

The kids listened and they kept sharing, and when they left the hotel and got home the parents were fighting. The kids were like, "Stop fighting and calm down." They breathed in and out and then they went inside. And they all took a nap together.

The next day they went to the beach and it started to rain. They were upset. They went under an umbrella till the rain stopped, then they went to the store to buy each of them a stress toy.

ANGELO WILSON is a sixth grade student at Sandburg Middle School.

MYSTERY
AND
SUSPENSE
STORIES

THE LADY NEXT DOOR

●　●　●　●　●　●　●　●　●　●　●　●　●　●　●

LEVI ATHIAS

One night, a nine-year-old boy was taking a walk with his dog, his parents drinking cocoa in the house. He took his dog on a walk every day at night and they lived in a barn far from people. He always used to tell himself he was a two-time state champ track runner for his age when he was seven years old. At eight years old, he was a three-time state champion. So he could outrun anybody if they tried to kidnap him. The dog stopped to sniff a plant when the boy realized there was a house in the distance. The boy thought to himself it couldn't hurt to check it out, as he walked closer he noticed the door was creaked open. The boy yelled in a curious way, "Anybody there?" As he expected, nobody answered. As he walked closer he noticed a large figure crawling around the house. As he fell back out of fear he lost grip of his dog and the dog went into the house and disappeared.

He did not want to go into the house but he knew his parents would kill him if they knew he had lost the dog. He took a step in and then another after another until he heard the door shut behind him. He turned back and ran to the door but he realized he needed to find his dog. He heard whimpering, but then suddenly it stopped. He turned back, but he did not see what he expected. He saw an eight-foot-tall woman dressed in all white looking down at him with the widest smile and blood dripping from her face. He ran out

27

the door as fast as he could, faster than he ever had before. He looked back and realized he was at least eighty feet away from the house now but he saw her in the corner of his eye: the eight-foot woman cracking her knuckles, back, and head. The woman got on all fours and closed the gap– eighty, seventy, sixty, fifty, forty, thirty, twenty, ten, and now five feet away in at least five seconds, she caught him and in a blink of an eye his soul was gone.

The parents looked at the time and realized it should not take thirty minutes to take their dog on a walk. When they walked outside to see if he was out there, they saw his body on the ground. They burst into tears and were on their knees begging for it to be a dream but it wasn't a dream at all.

LEVI ATHIAS is a sixth grade student at Sandburg Middle School.

JERED 1995

••••••••••••••••

FERNANDA ZARAZUA ENRIQUEZ

My grandpa Jered passed away recently. It was not expected for him to pass this early. The police don't want to investigate. So I'm taking it into my own hands. I drove up to his cold, foggy lake house on Wednesday, October 3, 1995. I parked a couple streets down just to be safe. I walked up and went through the back door. I realized it was wide open. I also saw wet muddy footprints. I walked in and I got the heebie-jeebies! I walked to the kitchen and found scissors covered in blood just lying on the floor. Whoever did this is not trying to hide this. I put them in a plastic bag for further investigation. I walked farther into the house and I could just tell this house hadn't been in maintenance for a long time! As I walked farther and farther in, I saw peeling wallpaper. I felt like someone or something was watching me. It gave me a paranormal vibe. I heard creaking and footsteps upstairs so I ran up there! I saw my grandpa Jered. He had faked his DEATH!! But what about the blood or all the clues? How was this all planned?

"But how and why would you do this?" I asked him.

My grandpa Jered said, "I was tired of being left alone. I wanted attention."

"Well you could have asked or said something. I would have helped you move closer to us so you could spend more time with us and not be alone."

As soon as I finished my sentence, he ran away and into the deep dark woods. From that day on I never saw or heard from him again.

FERNANDA ZARAZUA ENRIQUEZ is a girl that goes to Sandburg Middle School. She lives in a house with her family in the city of New Hope. She loves *Lilo and Stitch*, and her favorite color is pink. If she goes to college, she would like to pursue the arts or be a reporter. She enjoys writing because it has the power to calm people down and relax them. In her free time she likes to spend it with friends and family. She likes to ice skate or to play soccer. Her favorite food is steak and her mom's cooking. She also has a dog in Mexico and it is a doberman.

HALLOWEEN NIGHT

· ● ● ● ● ● ● ● ● ● ● ● ● ● ● ●

JULIANNI WHITFIELD

Halloween night, at a gas station Jamal and Ta'quavion were getting some drinks. When Jamal was going to the cashier he noticed that she was a beautiful blonde girl. When they made eye contact he fell in love. Ta'quavion thought she was way out of Jamal's league. As the blonde girl was scanning the drinks, Jamal asked her out on a date. She was so excited because she never had a date before. Ta'quavion didn't like her because he was suspicious of her.

The day of Jamal's date, Ta'quavion didn't trust the girl one bit. Back at the gas station, Ta'quavion had seen scales on the blonde girl's skin. When Jamal left for the date, Ta'quavion was nervous for Jamal. When Jamal got to the restaurant, he saw the blonde girl waiting outside, so he opened the door for her. When they got inside she ordered a ton of food, then Jamal saw the blonde girl's scales, and got scared. Then Jamal went to the storage room to calm down. The blonde girl followed him, he got nervous. The girl showed that she was a monster, then she ate him. The blonde girl paid for the bill, then went back to the gas station waiting for her next victim.

JULIANNI WHITFIELD is a sixth grader at Sandburg Middle School.

ABANDONED HOSPITAL

KENNY T.

Breathe. My legs were shaking. My heart was thumping. The smell, with the combination of the rotten wood, flesh, and insulation, just made everything worse in this abandoned hospital. I heard a slight whisper, saying, "Come out. . ." and immediately froze in place. I turned around, only to see a simple, rusty vent dispensing a light, arid breeze. I continued forward, expecting worse. Then, I could've sworn I saw two eyes appear right next to me. I jolted, expecting the worst. . . Nothing.

Just a room, seemingly leading into the void. Although I was hesitant, I proceeded into the room. Shards of glass everywhere, with a broken window dispensing a rush of cold wind. My eye caught something on the bed. I shined my flashlight toward the thing. *Bones!* Just *bones!*

Then, suddenly, a rush of adrenaline hit me. And a rush of a feeling that *something is coming.* I tried to convince myself that all of this is just my insanity going up, but my insanity has already reached its peak. I just ran. The feeling of *something coming* is at its peak. I had to look back. So I did. And—

OH MY GOSH.
What is that **THING?**
It's so freaking **BIG!**
It's coming closer.
Oh no, **OH NO, OH-**

KENNY T. is a sixth grader from New Hope, Minn. He describes himself as a chaotic-neutral outgoing introvert. Kenny spends a lot of time gaming, and also likes basketball, swimming, soccer, and fishing.

THE TUNNEL

VALARY K.

It was a beautiful afternoon, and we decided to go visit my aunt. I was exhausted on the road and I eventually dozed off.

"Why is it taking so long?" I said.

"I am over this," my brother also said.

The road we were on was very old, and nobody ever really went there. My dad had previously used this road, at least that's what he said. We got closer to a tunnel, and unfortunately our car broke down. My aunt's place was close by, and the sun was getting lower and disappearing. We got out and went in toward the tunnel.

It was unusually very cold in the tunnel, and there was water everywhere on the ground. Suddenly I felt uneasy. My head started to spin and my whole body was covered in goosebumps and chills. I was scared. I looked down and saw little creatures that looked like mice. They were very tiny, with sharp teeth and fur covered bodies. The wind blew and the little creatures were no more. I had many questions but no answers to them, and that made me more anxious and scared. In a very short time, I found myself standing in an unknown place. There I was, standing in the middle of the room. The room had a stench, a rotten smell. I knew that someone or something was surely out to get me.

VALARY K. is a sixth grade student at Sandburg Middle School and she hates working. Her favorite part about writing is the brainstorming part of it and her least favorite part is the writing or typing. Her favorite day is Saturday and she goes to church and then sleeps right after. She likes food a lot and especially African cuisine. She wants to be an Anesthesiologist when she grows to be an adult.

THE DARK TRAIL

● ● ● ● ● ● ● ● ● ● ● ● ● ● ●

YANESSY MUÑOZ

One day, a girl was walking her dog down a dark trail in the woods, and she was having a good time. She noticed that an old man in his forties was following her everywhere she walked her dog. She started to get a bad feeling about him, so she decided to go home. He also followed her to the house, and he waited outside. But after a few hours he went away. It was getting dark out, so she took a shower, ate dinner, and went to bed. Then in the middle of the night, she heard glass break outside of her room. So she stayed in bed, scared, and called one of her friends. Then she fell asleep. She woke up the next morning and her dog was missing and all her money and stuff was gone. She called the police, but they never found the person who did it.

YANESSY MUÑOZ is a sixth grade student at Sandburg Middle School.

THE COLLAPSE

● ● ● ● ● ● ● ● ● ● ● ● ●

LOGAN

I was about to leave a party that my best friend invited me to at his mega sized mansion. I've always dreamed of living in one. I looked at my watch, and it was already 2 a.m. I am going to get in so much trouble. I hate walking home in the shivering night with everything dark except for the twinkling stars in the night sky. This is my worst nightmare and it is going to become real!

I found a note on the ground, blended with the black gravel. It was a small black note that had small little holes like a piece of cheese. I turned the note over and felt frozen. It had one word. . .

RUN!

I am scared for my life. I can feel my heart stop and my legs feel like broken sticks. I started to run, just like it said. It felt like I ran for at least a mile. I turned to make sure nothing was behind me. I blinked to make sure. After that split second, there were lights twinkling down the never ending road. I felt like it was coming for me.

I started to run again. I got deeper and deeper on the never ending road. Then, I felt a sharp pain in my head and I collapsed. I was screaming in the night sky hoping I would stay alive.

Seconds later. . . BLACK. I never was seen again.

LOGAN attends Sandburg Middle School and he is in sixth grade. He also plays basketball and baseball and is really good at them and enjoys them. One fun fact about him is he really likes math because he likes how things work out and find solutions.

UNKNOWN THINGS

• • • • • • • • • • • • • • •

KARSYN RADEMACHER

In the town called Frilly, there was an abandoned hospital. It was October 17, 1997, at midnight. There was a girl named Milo. She was thirteen years old. She was walking down a street, but then she saw a van following her. . .

She got knocked out and dragged into the van. She was brought to this abandoned hospital that had been abandoned for thirty-five years. When she woke up, she was in the hospital in a bed and she had very bad feelings. . .

She saw a seven-foot-tall black shadow across from her. She felt shattered when she saw it, and she heard screaming and crying in other rooms. She felt fear in her body but she said to herself, *This didn't feel real at all.* She was in sleep paralysis. She couldn't move. SHE WOKE UP IN THE SAME PLACE AS HER DREAMS. She felt goosebumps running down her spine when she saw the shadow with very sharp nails. THE SHADOW DRAGGED HER AND ATE HER BODY IN ONE WHOLE MOUTHFUL. Everyone was looking for her, including her family and the town. Nobody found her, and the shadow was still hungry. . .

KARSYN RADEMACHER has a lot of pets and lives in a house with a basement and a main floor. She really likes to type a lot or write. Karsyn doesn't really like to read unless she's in the mood to. She loves to eat food

and chill out for fun or play on her virtual reality. She mostly plays Gorilla Tag or Capuchin.

OBSESSED

• ● ● ● ● ● ● ● ● ● ● ● ● ●

MIMI

Erica was always a good kid but she was not that pretty in her parents' eyes. Erica's mom and dad left her on the streets, so she moved in with David. David and Erica were a happy couple but they had their problems. Erica had an 8-hour shift, while David was a stay-at-home boyfriend that was lazy. He would get needy when she was at work because he would do nothing but go to the couch, eat, watch TV, and lastly go to the gym and then get back when Erica would come back. He would always tell her to change because her short sleeve shirt was too revealing and her skirt or pants would be too short.

David would complain each night that she would go to work and leave him there at home. She would always be quiet, go to her room and cry herself to sleep. But one night she did not do what she would do all of the time. Erica stood up for herself and started talking back. They had a heated argument that went on for hours. They were about to fight but then Erica said, "LEAVE MY HOUSE!!"

She started throwing his stuff out and started yelling at him about all the bad stuff he had done. With that she kicked him out and told him to never speak to her again. So he never came back to the house, but he came back to the streets. There were times she would randomly feel a shiver in her spine and goose bumps would appear all over her body. She

had never felt that feeling before she would only feel sad and happy and other positive emotions. The constant anxiety she felt whenever she stepped out of the house was becoming so unbearable that now she would only go outside to go to work and buy food.

Until one day her friend convinced her to go out with them and another boy named Eric. When they met they knew it was love at first sight and they started falling for each other a lot and Erica started going out—becoming easier prey. Eric and Erica started dating and soon got engaged. Their wedding was going to be on October 26, 2015. They lived happily together for the time being and would go out often. David would text her but she didn't notice because she was so excited in her new life that she forgot about him.

. . .

Erica

I started getting messages from an unknown number. I didn't know who it was, so I just ignored them. At one point I got annoyed because they would pop up every day. I decided to call the number because maybe it was someone I knew. So I called them and remembered it was David. I was annoyed that he had contacted me after I specifically told him to never talk to me again and hung up.

And with that I blocked him and erased him from my life. It was October 23. In three days, I would finally get married to Eric, the love of my life. I'm thankful that I went with my friend to hang out that day.

. . .

David

I was stalking Erica as usual but when I heard that she was getting married in three days my blood boiled. I thought

about things I could do to ruin the wedding and then the
perfect idea popped up. I was thinking of that while stalking
her then I noticed she was going to a house. The house was
beautiful and big. She saw a dude she called Eric then they
were talking about their wedding and that, that was their last
time together until the wedding.

Erica

I was walking to Eric's house. Finally I got there, we got his
stuff and went to the park for a picnic. It was so nice we kissed,
ate, and played old songs from our first date. We were about
to leave but then someone grabbed my hand and stopped me
from going. It was David, I was shocked that he was there. I
told him to back up, but he didn't back off.

At that time Eric took David's hand off of me and we were
leaving. But then David screamed "WE'LL MEET AGAIN
SOON." When he said that, I was confused but I just ignored it. Since I thought he was just trying to be a bad person. I really only remembered a little about him so I thought
he was not that bad.

I thought that he was just the type who did those things
but really never did anything bad. And with all of that happening Eric and I left for his house. We played games and
watched a movie until I had to leave. It felt like it went by
so fast, I didn't want to leave but there was no choice. So I
left and couldn't wait for the wedding. We locked eyes with
each other before we left and I wanted to run up to him but
I knew I couldn't.

. . .

Time had passed and it was now the day of the wedding.
Erica and Eric were so excited since they felt like they had
not seen each other for a while. Erica was walking down the
aisle, when a person showed up in all black with a black mask
with blonde hair sticking out. Everyone was shocked and

wondered who it was, even Eric. Eric came running to Erica but the masked man took her.

ERIC

I felt like I was waiting for eternity for Erica to arrive at the wedding. Once she was there I was so happy. She looked so beautiful in her dress, and I was ready to kiss her. Until I saw someone behind her grab her and look around the place. I went running to her but they saw and ran away.

They were really fast so I couldn't catch up to them. They took her and I started crying because I couldn't catch up to them to save her. The thing that hurt me the most were her screams. I felt so bad about the whole situation.

ERICA

I was walking down the aisle with my dad until someone pushed him down and grabbed my arm. I didn't know who they were. I was looking around until Eric came running to me. I thought I was saved until the random person took me out of the room. They put a bag around my head and I could barely breathe. They put me in a car from what I could feel and hear from the engine starting.

It felt like the drive was so long until we finally got there. Because they picked me up roughly and put me in a chair. They tied up my hands, feet and waist. They took the bag off of my face and felt like I could finally breathe. After breathing at an average speed I tried to figure out who it was.

Until they spoke and told me something they took off their mask and it was David. I was shocked but not that much. I really thought that what he said was just a sick joke. But I mean now I know that he was not joking and I asked him why he did that.I was mad since it was my wedding day.

He said it was because of me. I was confused until he kissed me. I felt mad I was trying to kick him or move my head away from him. But he was too strong so couldn't get

away from him. Until he relaxed more than I took my opportunity to get away from him. I was left breathing heavily because, not gonna lie, that kiss lasted for a minute.

He said that I'll be his but I told that I would never be his. He got mad when I said that so he put the bag back on my head and left. And with that I was left in the dark screaming for someone so come.

DAVID

I was sick and tired of Erica because she was being annoying. So I put the bag back on her head and turned off the lights. I was trying to watch tv because Erica was in the basement so I was waiting for her to go to sleep. Until she started to scream for help and I was fed up with it. So I went into the basement to shut her up, and once I said that, she was shut up for good.

· · ·

At last Erica fell asleep so David took her to her room. He put her on a chair and tied her up there. When she woke up she just passed out because she was really frightened. She heard someone coming into the room. She was so happy when she saw Eric standing by the door about to run to her.

Eric came to David's house and tried to go in. He succeeded in getting in so he saw her and was going to free her but David came. David ran to the kitchen then back. He pinned Eric to the wall and was going to beat him but he escaped. Erica fainted from the shock of what happened.

David went to check on Erica but that was when she had just passed out. So he tried to wake Erica up and it worked. She was still afraid but not enough to pass out. When she woke up David was putting a chain on her leg and then untied her. He said, " You can walk around the house, but if you try to leave or to take off the chain I'll put you back on the bed".

She was really shaky so she just nodded and left the room.

She went to go eat since she had not eaten but Daivd stopped her and cooked the food for her. David was rich because of his dad's death so he had maids who were really nice. And David started to be nicer than usual with Erica.

One day, David really thought that Erica was being good, so he planned to go on a date with her. Erica was really excited because it was her first time outside after six months. On the date, they were hiking and she nearly died from falling off a cliff. But thankfully David saved her before that happened. She was not actually scared, but she pretended to be scared so she could go to the bathroom. When she got there, she actually didn't use the bathroom. She was planning what to use and thinking about how to escape. She finally thought of a plan and put it to work. She did her plan successfully and escaped.

After Erica was not there, David went to go look for her. But she wasn't there. He looked for her for days, but David couldn't find her.

MIMI has two pet guinea pigs named Shoyo and Mochi. She lives in Minnesota in a Mexican community with her mom, dad, and three siblings. Her favorite food is rice and boiled egg. Her favorite sport is either volleyball or badminton. A fun fact about her is that she can play the flute.

THE COFFEE SHOP

Harper Wulff

As I walk in the coffee shop, the strong smell of rotten wood blows around. The wind comes in from the window with the cold breeze. Cobwebs hover over me as I walk. I turn around... I see a bloody hand in a blender. Shivering with coldness, blood drips down the walls. The floor is creaking as I slowly walk. Then, a lullaby starts to play. I pull my sleeves down. I feel the chills go slowly through my body.

I see where the sound is coming from, an old disc player. As I turn around I notice another door. The door creaks as I open it. Bloody clothes are all over the floor, a finger in a jar, a bloody knife in a dirty sink. As I turn my head, I see a secret passage half covered by a box. I slowly turn the knob of the passage, and see stairs leading down with red carpet. The stairs creak as I go down them, with dust and cobwebs everywhere. As I approach the bottom, I see a room that looks perfectly normal, but as I keep walking I see lots of doors with numbers one through six.

I open the first door and it's something that looks like a jail cell. I see a human laying on the floor dead! I start breathing heavily with all the nerves in my body tingling. I turn around and slowly shut the door. Do I dare open another? But when I hear someone coming down the stairs, I quickly hide behind a chair. I see them in all black with a hood and a

mask on! He turns the news on. What am I going to do? He gets up and walks into door four. I will make a run for it! I get out and keep running and running.

Two weeks later the coffee shop was investigated and the man was put in jail and never heard from him again.

HARPER WULFF is a sixth grader from New Hope, Minn. She enjoys playing hockey and hanging out with her friends.

LUNA THE DOCTOR

- - - - - - - - - - - - - - - -

JOHNATTA R. MITCHELL

Once upon a time, in a town called The Green Village, there was a girl called Luna. She was a very smart girl and she lived with her parents. Luna loved to read, but one day her family was killed by the town chief. She and her mother were the only ones who survived it. But Luna did not give up on her dream. Five years later, Luna graduated from college and became a doctor.

Luna was a successful doctor. She got married to a police officer and gave birth to beautiful twin girls. A month later, Luna's mother got sick, so Luna took her mother to her hospital. When they got there, they did all of Luna's mother's tests. They found out she had cancer and she only had ten months to live. So Luna spent as much time as she could with her mother before her mother died.

After ten months, Luna's mother did not die. When they went back to the hospital, the nurse said, "I'm sorry madam, we mixed your mother's result with someone else's result. Your mother's lungs have a problem, but we have the cure to it."

Luna and her family were very happy. They all danced and sang for the life of their mother, and they all lived happily ever after.

JOHNATTA R. MITCHELL is a sixth grade student at Sandburg Middle School.

UPSIDE DOWN ZOMBIE HORROR

●‍●‍●‍●‍●‍●‍●‍●‍●‍●‍●‍●‍●‍●‍●‍●

ADELINE BERNHAUER

I was walking down the street to meet my friend. It was dark and cloudy outside. I stopped short when I heard an obnoxious groaning gurgling noise behind me. I turned around, all I saw was an empty road behind me. I thought I was just hearing things, so I kept walking.

I heard the noise again. This time I did not look back. I started to run. I ran into a hotel. It was super dark. It smelled moldy and moist. Then I saw a beat-up man. He looked like my friend, except he was green and scary. He started to run after me! I quickly left the hotel and ran towards the woods.

I kept running and my head was in circles! The leaves behind me were crunching from me and the zombie. Then I realized he might be a zombie! I started to run even faster! Then before I thought things couldn't get worse, I heard a thump. I realized I tripped over a log! My friend came closer and I thought he wouldn't hurt me. He was my friend. . . Right? He came closer. He grabbed me and bit me! It hurt so bad I let out a horrendous scream! Then everything went blank. . .

ADELINE BERNHAUER is a sixth grade student at Sandburg Middle School.

THE FOOTSTEPS

ALYSSA GOERTS

It was a dark, cold, and rainy night. Lexi couldn't sleep, so she put on her coat and snuck out of the house to go on a walk. When she started walking down the street she heard a car pull up behind her. She heard leaves crunching and footsteps. Lots of footsteps. She swung herself around just to see. . . Nothing? Nothing but a cold dark street with puddles of water. She thought it was just her imagination so she kept walking.

After about 15 minutes of walking she decided to head back home. Then she heard a sickening, terrifying scream from behind her. It sounded close. Lexi jumped and started sprinting back home. She kept looking back hoping nobody was chasing or following her.

Lexi stopped in her tracks. She looked up and there, right in front of her, was a tall man in a black sweatshirt. The man had a piece of what looked to be a wire from a fence but whatever it was it looked sharp. Lexi screamed and the man started walking towards her. Lexi was running for her life but she didn't know where she was. All she knew was that she should keep running. She didn't know how long she had been running but she was probably far away from home. She frantically looked around to find anything to know where she was. She didn't know what time it was but the sun started to come up. Then she heard a voice yelling " Lexi! Lexi!" It

was her dad! She saw her dad's car. He got out of the driver's seat and hugged her. "What were you doing out here?" he asked. Lexi told him the whole story about sneaking out and the man with the wire. Then they went home. Lexi never came across the man again but every now and then when she is outside she will hear some faint footsteps behind her.

ALYSSA GOERTS is a sixth grader at Sandburg Middle School. She lives in New Hope, Minn.

THE FACTORY

NATHAN KELLY

One day on February 31, I was taking a midnight stroll, when I saw an abandoned factory that had never been there before. I decided that I would head in. The cool wind hit my neck as I headed in. The factory was larger than I expected.

I was inspecting the machines, when I heard a loud banging. I tensed up, and I went to investigate. There was a figure standing next to a person on the ground. The figure hadn't seen me yet. He just stood there with a bat and his mask, smiling menacingly.

I took a picture of the person so I could show the police, but when I looked back, the man was gone. Now I couldn't show the police; they would think I did it. Where did this villain go? He couldn't be far, but I knew I had to get out of here. Something strange was going on here, and my head started to buzz like fluorescent lights. Everything started to buzz. It was mad. I headed toward the exit, but when I jiggled the door, it wouldn't budge. As I looked further in the factory, the buzzing got worse like something was calling me. I shivered and zipped up my coat. The building was cracked here, but I still headed deeper into the building. I started to sweat.

Then I saw him, the guy who hurt the person on the floor just from before. He just stood there. He seemed different

though. He seemed to shake. Maybe I didn't notice before, but he was shaking like he was scared of something. I didn't know what to do now. So I threw a rock next to him, and he didn't move. I did it again, and he didn't move. I finally got the courage to go over there, and he still didn't move. The buzzing started to hurt as I was getting closer to whatever was buzzing. I got closer to something that looked like veins in a human body. Was the building alive? I had to investigate. Then out of nowhere, something hit me over the head, and I was knocked out. It was the guy with the mask. He threw me out of the building, and it disappeared when I looked back. Even now, five years later, it's still hard to believe.

NATHAN KELLY is a sixth grader from New Hope, Minn. Nathan has two dogs and one cat. His favorite food is rice and he loves to play with his friends.

THE ONLY HAUNTED HOUSE

* * * * * * * * * * * * * *

CLEMY TSHIBANDA

I was walking down a spooky forest when I unexpectedly saw an immense moldy brown house. The windows were shattered, and the door was creaking. I was very curious, so then I walked up the front steps and decided to take a look. I slowly went inside. . . then BOOM!

The door slammed right behind me, and the lights started to flicker. My skin started to slither, my heart was pumping so fast, and I was breathing very heavily. I was trying not to panic but. . . the lights just went out. . . until I remembered I had a flashlight in my backpack. I quickly opened up my backpack, and brought out my flashlight.

The wind blowing from the windows, the heavy rain, and the thunder in the background made me terrified. I quickly zipped up my backpack, and saw a few stairs that led to a basement. I stared right down at the stairs, and turned on my flashlight. And right there, I saw a horrendous skeleton that was dead. It seemed to be eleven feet tall. My heart was racing as fast as the wind that blew my hair. I was breathing so heavily that I thought that I might pass out. My brain was telling me to fight it, but my heart was telling me to run and leave the skeleton alone. I went with my heart. My flashlight was going to run out soon, but the windows were shattered, and

then I had an idea. I grabbed a random wrench I found on the floor and broke open the window. I quickly went out the window with my backpack on my back, and my flashlight. Because I remembered it was in my hand, I was relieved.

CLEMY TSHIBANDA is a sixth grade student at Sandburg Middle School. She lives in New Hope, Minn.

THE PLANE RIDE

MATEO DIAZ JIMENEZ

I was on a plane to visit my family. The plane ride was about three hours so it wasn't that long. . . or so I thought. One hour into the plane ride, I heard some noise. I didn't know what it was since almost everyone on the plane was asleep. I looked at the people sitting next to me and they were sleeping so then I went to the restroom.

When I got out of the restroom I heard a voice say, "Hey! Why is everyone asleep?"

I turned around and saw a man close to his late 30s. I said, "I didn't know!"

Then the plane started to shake like crazy. He and I held onto some seats and when the plane settled, I asked him "What's your name?"

He replied, "My name is Zack! And yours?"

I said, "My name is Hendrix, nice to meet you."

Then out of nowhere we heard crying but it felt far away. So there we were trying to find the person who was crying but then when I looked at one person sleeping in their seat they opened their eyes and I got scared for a second.

Then Zack said, "Hey, man! You good?"

I said, "Yeah," and then the lights to the plane turned off and then. . . I heard a bone-chilling sound of what seemed like low pitched screaming. Then I looked behind me and I saw a very tall person—so tall that they towered over me.

Then I started to run. I yelled to Zack to run to the restroom. He opened the door to the restroom. He and I got into the restroom.

Zack said "Bro, what happened?" I was scared. I didn't know what to say then I heard a woman say, "Hello. Is there someone in there?"

Zack opened the door and we saw a woman but when she saw us both in the restroom she just walked away. When Zack and I got out of the restroom, it was like nothing happened.

Zack said, "What did you see?"

I said, "I saw a tall person but I didn't know."

Zack said, "I don't think they were human."

I said, "Yeah you're right!"

Then we heard the pilot say, "All right everyone get back to your seats we are about to land."

I got back to my seat and sat down. Shortly after, the plane landed.

MATEO DIAZ JIMENEZ is a sixth grade student at Sandburg Middle School. He lives in Golden Valley, Minn.

FRIDAY THE 13TH, 2016

● ● ● ● ● ● ● ● ● ● ● ● ● ● ● ●

ASEEL HIHI

Once, I was telling my friend Lavaria about this time I went to this abandoned mall. You may be asking why I went to an abandoned mall. Well, let me tell you the whole story.

It was November 13th, 2016 and it was also. . . Friday the 13th. I was with my friends Sadie, April, Chamauri, and Lilly. They were all at my house and wanted to do something exciting and spooky. Me and my friends were all brainstorming some ideas and then Lilly said we should go to an abandoned mall. I said yes and so did Chamauri, Sadie, and April. We were all very excited but first we would have to get our moms to agree. All of us knew our moms would not agree so we just said it was a regular mall and they said yes. As I was walking to the abandoned mall with my friends, I realized I didn't bring money so I asked Chamauri if she brought money. She said no. Then, we asked Sadie she also said no. Finally, we asked Lilly and she said no too! I was sure April brought some but she also forgot! I couldn't ask mom to bring us money because we were almost at the abandoned mall and I knew we would get in trouble. We just decided why would we need money if it's abandoned? It's not like we're gonna be able to buy anything.

Then we arrived at the abandoned mall at 5:30 p.m., and it was very spooky. We saw some spider webs which were disgusting! We got on the escalator which wasn't running so we took the stairs. Once we got on the second floor, we heard some suspicious noises but thought nothing of it. We continued exploring the mall and we ran into a Forever 21. There were still lots of clothes in there and we decided to go in. When Me, Lilly, Sadie, April, and Chamauri were looking at the clothes, we realized they were really cute. Since nobody was there we decided we were just gonna take them without paying. I mean, who would care? We got the clothes, took some bags to put our clothes in, and we tried to go find another store with a lot of clothes. But as I was walking with my friends I started to hear some weird sounds again. I asked my friends but they all said no. . . I then thought I was just imagining stuff. I kept on walking but then I heard another sound but this time it wasn't just me. My friends heard it too! It was loud and we were not sure what it was.

Chamauri said she thought it might be a person and I agreed. Lilly seemed very anxious and didn't say much. Sadie said, "Is anybody there?" and nobody replied. Then we realized that April was gone! We all started shouting, "April where are you?" and, "April where did you go?!" We all started to get really scared and decided we should split up and go look for April. Chamauri and I went to look for her on one side of the mall then Sadie and Lilly went the other way. Lilly said, "Aseel, are you sure we should split up?" I said yes, and so did Chamauri and Sadie. Chamauri and I went right and Sadie and Lilly went left. Chamauri and I couldn't find April anywhere and decided we were gonna go back and meet up with Lilly and Sadie. I touched my pocket to grab my phone and call Lilly but then realized I have no connection. Then Chamauri tried to call Lilly but she also had no connection. Still, we both tried to call Sadie and couldn't. We had no idea what we were gonna do but then we decided we were just

gonna go look for them so me and Chamauri were walking around yelling, "LILLY, SADIE WHERE ARE YOU?!?"

Then we heard a scream! We all got grounded for a long time. Lilly got grounded for a week. April got grounded for a month. I got grounded for 2 months and Chamauri is still grounded to this day. The end.

Lavaria says, "You're definitely lying, Aseel. There's no way that's a real story!" I say, "Yes it is, but believe what you wanna believe."

Aseel Hihi is a sixth grade student at Sandburg Middle School.

OCTOBER 31ST

● ● ● ● ● ● ● ● ● ● ● ● ● ● ●

CHAMAURI PENDLETON

It was the day before October 31st, 1999. I heard knocking at my door at 2:30 am on the 31st of October. I opened the door very slowly hoping I wasn't gonna get jump-scared. Turns out I didn't. It was just Val and Markiya. I was still in my pajamas. I didn't even get time to change. Val and Markiya pulled me out of the doorframe. We headed to the abandoned hospital with a flashlight and walkie-talkie. We finally arrived. All I saw was mist everywhere. I could barely see. We walked all around the hospital to find an entrance. We finally found one. As soon as we entered, I felt a cold breeze across my face which gave me chills. Out of nowhere came a dark figure standing in front of us. The figure pointed in different directions but the figure told me to follow it so I did. We were walking down the hallway for three whole hours. I know that because I got bored and started counting. I wonder where they are right now. The figure stopped and went to the room on its left and I followed. By the time I entered the room the figure was gone. I was all alone. I'd been walking for so long. I knew I couldn't go back. I'd gone too far. Now I was starting to think we shouldn't have split up. I stopped. I heard loud screams knowing my friends were gone. I was all alone. I heard noises behind me and when I turned around it was the black figure I had followed. It jumped at me and. . .

I GUESS THERE WAS NO HAPPY ENDING FOR
US ALL... EVEN THE FIGURE.

CHAMAURI PENDLETON is a sixth grade student at
Sandburg Middle School. Her favorite sport is basketball. The thing Chamauri finds hardest about writing
is having to think of stuff off the top of her head and
it having to relate to what the story is supposed to be
about. Chamauri would love to make it to UCLA.

THIS TIME I MET MYSELF, BUT IN THE FUTURE

● ● ● ● ● ● ● ● ● ● ● ● ● ● ●

Bo Crouse

I was *really* bored one day. I was scrolling through Google Maps, but then I found a children's abandoned psych ward. I was looking for something, *anything*, to do. I looked up the directions and it was only fifteen minutes away! I was like, "I'M TOTALLY DOING THIS." I felt a little uneasy about it, like something terrible was going to happen. I brought up the directions and walked there.

When I got there, it looked like it had been abandoned for at least 10 years. The feeling was *very* uneasy. It was *very* dark. I went inside and anything that I stepped on creaked. I heard a voice say, "Are you here to save me?" I thought I was hallucinating but after that, I saw something run in front of me. I felt *SO HORRIFIED* I could not scream or move, then I saw it again. I felt a chill and I wanted to scream.

A figure came up and I saw it. It was a little 8-year-old girl. She said: "HAHA I GOT YOU, YOU WERE SCARED." I was frozen, then I said "H-Hi." She was like "I'm Lily and I scare everyone out of here, but you must be fearless." She was so sweet. I met a few others, like Alexander. He showed me

his friends. They were all so nice and many more, I only met a few out of, like, *a lot*. I met a girl. She gave me a teddy bear and insisted it was mine. She kept saying: "I was waiting for you, this *is* yours." I took it because I felt bad. I went home to wash it but I noticed the tag. I was shook. IT. WAS. MY. NAME. The child was me.

BO CROUSE is a sixth grade student at Sandburg Middle School. Axel has a dog named Toast and really likes boba. Axel does have ADHD, which is hard but it also is helpful at times.

JOURNEY OF THE DEAD

● ● ● ● ● ● ● ● ● ● ● ● ● ● ●

KENZIE SCHLACHTER

I t all started one night at 11 p.m., at Alex's house. His best
friend Bailey and him were playing video games like always and fell asleep. Some knocking started at the door
and intensified by the second. Eventually Alex got up from
the noise, and checked the cameras. Oddly enough, nobody
was there. . . But he was so tired he just shrugged it off and
went back to sleep. The next morning, Bailey woke up and
checked her phone. *8:15 a.m.*

"Ah! Alex, wake up! We're gonna be late for school!" she
yelled. They both ran to get dressed and grab their bikes.
They got to school and ran inside but something was. . . different. All the lights were out and everyone was gone. No
teachers. No students. Empty. Alex spied a flickering light
near a line of windows.

"Hey. . . do you see that?" he said pointing.
"Hmmm." Bailey ran over and turned the light on to see claw
marks on the wall. She jumped back in surprise and knocked
Alex over. They were getting really freaked out now and were
wondering if this was a prank. Bailey saw a shadow coming
from the window. She slowly opened the blinds with a drop
of sweat on her forehead. Alex grabbed a garbage lid and held
it as a shield just in case, but they were surprised to see that all
that was outside was a street.

"Huh, guess I was imagining things, maybe we should just

go home," Bailey insisted. Just as they were grabbing their bikes from the lot, Alex screamed and Bailey quickly turned to see him missing.

"Alex? Hello?!" She started to panic when she realized he wasn't responding anywhere. She started to run around looking for him and heard a whimpering from an ally.

Bailey turned into the ally and saw Alex laying on the ground holding his arm as blood dripped from under his hand here and there. She felt her heart stop and face turn pale.

"OH MY GOD ALEX, WHAT HAPPENED?" she screamed. But he still wasn't responding. His pupils dilated back to normal and he stumbled to his feet quickly.

"Bailey, listen to me right now, run as fast as you can back home, leave your bike, leave everything, just run." Tears started streaming from Bailey's eyes and she tried to wake him back up after he silenced again but he was gone. He would never be the same and she was about to find out why...

KENZIE SCHLACHTER is a sixth grade student at Sandburg Middle School. She likes to sketch, paint, and play the violin. Mackenzie loves space and wants to be an astrophysicist when she's older. She loves all food but as an Italian, her favorites are ravioli and mac 'n cheese.

THE TRAP

JACOB SOLOMON

It was a dark, abandoned mall. But I had to run away. I walked into the mall and the door was locked. I heard someone walking behind me but when I looked no one was there.

I walked past a store and saw the police outside. I hid in a candy store. Then I saw a Pez dispenser fall over. I didn't think about it though. I felt like there was something watching me but I had to hide so I went into the bathroom.

When I went there, there was a BEAR TRAP! I jumped over it but then there was a noise that made me jump. I fell back and fell into the bear trap. Now my leg is caught in the bear trap, my leg hurt very badly then I saw a Pez dispenser. All of the Pez dispensers surrounded me and they started to eat me.

JACOB SOLOMON is a sixth grader at Sandburg Middle School. He lives in Crystal, Minn.

WHERE'S RACHEL

●　●　●　●　●　●　●　●　●　●　●　●　●　●

SOPHIA XIONG

Y ou and your friend, Felicity, were having the night of
your lives. . . or so you thought. You two were hanging out and doing whatever until Felicity asked where
Rachel was. Rachel told you guys that she'd be back after going out for fresh air.

Rachel had been gone for over 20 minutes already and
Felicity was searching the whole house. You decided to go
head outside and ask anybody if they knew about her where-
abouts. After another ten minutes of asking, you've found
out that she went toward the corn fields that were near the
house where the party took place.

You were hesitant at first. Since the corn fields are pretty
huge. But, you and Felicity decided to do it. After all, Rachel
and you two were inseparable best friends. If something had
happened to her in the corn field, you would regret not going
for the rest of your life.

You and Rachel came up with an agreement that you two
would be sticking together the whole time in that corn field.
You took a humongous flashlight out for our search along
with us. It was pitch black and I felt my body trembling every
single step we'd take.

Along with your search, you started becoming paranoid
and had started to hear sounds. You thought it was from
your imagination until Felicity stated that she was hearing

some sounds, too. The sound was of crunching leaves, that kept creeping closer, and closer every single step you'd take. You broke out in a sweat as you wondered, "Are we both imagining this? Am I overthinking?"

All of a sudden, heavy breathing followed with the footsteps you had been hearing. Louder and louder the panting sound came. You and Felicity looked right at each other, and started running. As you ran, all you could think was, "Don't look back, just RUN." You just wanted to get away from that thing, or whatever it was.

You came to a stop, at least for now. Looking around, you were finally safe. But Felicity wasn't with you, the ONE thing you two agreed on. Obviously, you're relieved that you're not hurt, but at the same time, worried for the sake of not only Rachel, but now Felicity. The only thing you wanted now was for them to be safe.

After a while of searching for an exit, you found one. "Finally, at last!" you whispered to yourself. You don't know how much time has passed, but it was still dark out. The exit you found had led into the woods. The trees swayed from the light breeze as they blocked out any sort of light trying to come through. It was pitch black in the corn fields, and now in the woods.

You proceeded into the woods, wandering around but making sure to keep track of your surroundings and steps. You were following a pathway as well, wondering if it even led to somewhere. Creeping along through the woods, there was a stop. There were two paths you could choose from, one of them leading to death (except you didn't know that, of course). You choose the left pathway and follow along it.

Questioning yourself if it was safe, you continued as usual with anxious thoughts flooding through your mind. While glancing to the side, you saw a little light peeking through the branches of the trees. It wasn't connected to the pathway, but you went over anyway. After almost tripping on the

leaves and sticks on the ground, you made it to the end of where the light came from.

Going near it, everything turned into a bright light. You were surrounded by the light. No more darkness. You didn't know what was happening, but you felt at peace. No more worries, no more wandering, nothing.

It turns out that you DIED. On the search for Rachel, you and Felicity never came out of that corn maze, and it was all in your head. You passed out and had been guided out to heaven, where your soul lies in peace. But... we'll never know where Rachel is.

SOPHIA XIONG is a sixth grade student at Sandburg Middle School.

THE HOUSE IN THE ALLEY

Thomas Rowan

You and your friend Marshall are just chilling in your house in New York. When you look out the window, you see a house that has been abandoned for months. You and your friend argue on who has to go. Short story, you lost. You run down the stairs and out the door. You cross the street and then you are at the door of the house. You enter slowly and see tons of papers with blood smeared across them. Then, you hear MONSTERS screeching and you sprint out of the house. You run back in and see that the papers are the history of the house. You collect all the papers you can see, then the monsters start running towards you. You sprint to the door and barely make it out alive. You run back to your house and discuss the information with Marshall. You find out that the house was overtaken by monsters, and you also find out that everybody on earth has to go in the house and if you find out that the monsters will kill you if you take too long gathering information. You see you have stumbled upon a death game. But you see the prize for whoever can win gets whatever they want for all of existence. You don't want to die, but you also want to win.

Knowing you will have to go in eventually you take your shot. You run back into the house with Marshall, and with

help from Marshall you find keys and unlock rooms and find more papers until you are down to the last room. The monsters are staring right at you, but all you have to do is get the music player, and get out, then you win. But the monsters are guarding it, and you have a feeling that this will be a big fight. Marshall runs in and gets the music player, throws it to you, and then he holds them off, and then you run out while Marshall gets killed. You don't know what to do and a genie comes out of the music player. The music player announces that you have beat the death game and you will get everything you will ever want for all of eternity. You are shocked and speechless. But you realize that whatever doesn't kill you, only makes you stronger.

THOMAS ROWAN has two cats, Oliver and Lucky. He lives with my siblings and parents. And he lives in a house in New Hope, Minn. He loves pizza because it is just so enjoyable to eat. His favorite sport is dance and he also loves to do math. His favorite way to spend a Saturday is probably just to relax.

THE TALL, SLENDER FIGURE

MIATTA MILLIGAN

It was slowly getting dark and I didn't know where I was. It seemed like a hospital, but it looked abandoned and smelled rotten—like someone died in here. As I continued deeper into the building, I heard a scratching sound. I slowly looked around with my hands trembling. I shined the flashlight in the direction where I heard the sound and I felt something grab me by my leg, trying to drag me. I tried to free myself but the grip on my leg was too strong. But suddenly whatever grabbed me loosened its grip. Once I freed myself I quickly ran the other direction, trying to escape. When I felt that I was far enough, I started gasping for air while my lungs froze from the cold air. After I caught my breath, I started realizing I dropped my flashlight in terror. Not knowing where I was, I looked at the dark night sky. After I built up the courage to go back I slowly went the other way looking for my flashlight.

As I went to look for my flashlight, trying to see what's ahead of me, my foot got caught on a rope. I noticed there were a lot more broken windows in this area. After walking more, I finally found my flashlight and let out a heavy sigh as I checked to see if my flashlight was damaged. Luckily it wasn't, but I did see something red on the ground. It looked

exactly like blood. I covered my mouth in terror. I soon calmed myself down knowing my imagination can make me overthink. But suddenly I felt someone watching me. I looked around terrified.

"Is someone there?" I called out but I heard nothing for a few seconds.

Later, I heard a short growling noise and I realized that I wasn't alone. Actually I might have been scared, but I never chicken out. I went in the direction of the noise (which was on the second floor) with my flashlight clenched tightly in my hands feeling braver than ever. Hearing the sound of broken glass crunching as I walked didn't make me feel any safer, but I kept calling out. The noises got louder and louder, almost like an ear-bleeding scream and crying sound when I reached the room. The sound was coming from what seemed like a small child in the corner wailing. As I walked over to the child, it looked at me but had no face, just black where the face was supposed to be. I stepped back in a panic trying to collect my thoughts. Whatever I saw started growing—or should I say changing—into a tall, slender figure. I tried to run away but the figure grabbed me and I saw nothing but black.

Did my life really end like this? It did.

MIATTA MILLIGAN is a sixth grade student at Sandburg Middle School.

THE LAB

● ● ● ● ● ● ● ● ● ● ● ● ● ● ●

KENZOE HEARN

One day, a boy named Jamal was skateboarding to his friend's house. They were planning to go to the skatepark together. He knocked on the door, and then it opened. No one was there. He walked in and quietly said, "Hello?" He heard his voice echo, but there was no response. He repeated, a little louder this time, "Hello?" He heard the screech of a door upstairs. He started going up the stairs. Once he reached the top, he saw a door to a room cracked open slightly.

He slowly started to step towards the door. As he was getting closer, he noticed that the room looked bright. Like it led to something. He opened the door fully, and what he saw shocked him. It was a government molecular converter. He looked around, and all he saw was a bunch of plexiglass rooms with people in them. These weren't normal people though. They looked almost dead, and he wasn't sure why. But he knew for sure that something bad was happening.

Jamal wanted to investigate, but he was afraid that he would end up like these people. The other thing that confused him the most was that this door was in his friend's house. And his friend wasn't home. So that could only mean . . . his friend could be one of these people.

Jamal didn't wanna get killed, so he turned back only to see the door was gone. His heart dropped. He was gonna be here

forever unless He could find a way out and back home. But there was no chance. He didn't even know if he was awake or dreaming at this point. He was about to find somewhere to hide when he heard an alarm and saw red lights throughout the whole building.

Now Jamal really had to hide. He looked around, but he didn't see anything. He saw a door, and then ran to it. It was locked. Then, over the sirens, he heard a computer voice saying, "Security breach," and, "Test chambers." He thought to himself, "This must be the test chamber." How did it know I was here though?

Jamal looked at the door again and saw men in full body-suits made of rubber and plastic. They were running towards this door. He had to hide fast! He ran around the whole room looking for a spot to hide. I saw one of the test chambers was open. Jamal didn't wanna go in there knowing the risk of getting trapped. The door started opening, so it was his only choice.

KENZOE HEARN is a sixth grade student at Sandburg Middle School.

TONIGHT IS HALLOWEEN

● ● ● ● ● ● ● ● ● ● ● ● ● ●

ISABELLE LINK

I just moved to a ghost town, and tonight is Halloween. I'm so excited. Oh, you might be thinking I'm trick-or-treating or handing out candy. No, no. I'm hosting a haunted house. I'm so lucky I got a mansion for a hundred dollars, but, then again, there have been multiple disappearances in it. I made my haunted house with a "lost in the woods" theme, so it will be scary—but not too scary. I hope the kids will like it, but still get scared. Hopefully no one will get nightmares.

Fast-forward to tonight: My haunted house is up and running. All of a sudden, the street fogs up. Doors open and creak loudly. I shiver, my heart beating fast. I run as fast as I can. I think about all the things this could be. Maybe a ghost? A curse? No, no, it can't be that. Those things aren't real. Maybe my new neighbors are just playing a prank on me.

No, if it was that, they all would have been planning earlier and not getting ready for tonight. What could this be? There has to be an explanation, but what is it? I wonder if it is a ghost because, I mean, these are all the signs of one. Could it be? No, this is crazy talk. What am I even saying? Ghosts aren't real. Wait, where's my phone?! How did I just realize

I haven't had it all day? Did I lose it? My life is going south today. Then I woke up and realized it was all just a dream.

Isabelle Link is a sixth grade student at Sandburg Middle School.

THE RP STORY

●·●·●·●·●·●·●·●·●·●·●·●·●

DAVARION JONES

So I'm at home, in my room playing Grand Theft Auto. I was playing GTA and my controller died. I changed the batteries and I joined a roleplay server in the game and went to the store and it got robbed. Someone was shooting glass bottles and glass shards went everywhere. I ran out the store.

So the guy that was shooting hit the pumps and my car blew up and I ran to the back of the gas station running to my house and I saw my homie's car. So I called him and told him to let me in and I told him what happened and he was in shock and then he dropped me off.

DAVARION "DJ" JONES is a sixth grader at Sandburg Middle School. He lives in Brooklyn Park, Minn.

THE HOUSE

●　●　●　●　●　●　●　●　●　●　●　●　●

APRIL RUIZ

Hi, I'm Elizabeth. I always wonder, *Am I real? What if my whole life is a dream?* I wake up and I'm a new thing or person. I don't know, maybe I'm just thinking too much.

I have two brothers who don't do anything in the house but stay in their room. My mom and dad work three jobs because of bills, food, and more. So I clean the whole house by myself.

One time when I went home, the house was a mess. I got so mad that I'm doing all the cleaning work, so I went to my brothers' room and I screamed, "GET UP AND HELP ME CLEAN BEFORE MOM AND DAD GET HERE!"

They yelled back "NO, I'M ABOUT TO BEAT THIS GAME!"

I yelled back, "YOU GUYS KNOW WHAT MOM AND DAD HAVE TO GO THROUGH FOR YOUR GAMES AND MUCH MORE. BUT YOU DON'T WANT TO DO ANYTHING FOR THEM YOU GUYS ARE SUCH LAZY PEOPLE!"

After that I just rushed to my room before they saw a tear. A tear means you're weak but sometimes you get so mad you just start to cry. I ran to my room and cried myself to sleep before my mom and dad could get here. I started to fall

asleep and I slept for thirteen hours. I woke up in the same room but something felt off.

I went out of my room to see a new house, there were so many rooms downstairs, upstairs, and basement. It was all clean. But when I went downstairs, it was dark so I looked outside and everything looked like a cartoon. I tried to open the door but it stuck and I couldn't get out. So I looked all over the house. There was a picture on the wall and it was me but when I was five with a girl, but her face was cut off. And my face, it was not normal. I could tell I did not look like that as a kid. And there was a book out of the bookshelf and it said "Help!" It had pictures of a lion and a sheep hugging and then I looked over to the corner of the house. There was a lion and sheep hugging and I remember that lion and sheep. I don't know how but I do. So I put the book back.

I know I need to get out of this house, so when I tried to open the front door it worked. I went out but when I took the first step out it brought me back into the house. I could only yell, "HELP. . . HELP. . ." I started breaking down into tears and I yelled, "HELP ME. PLEASE ANYONE *please.*"

Then I heard footsteps coming from upstairs and downstairs. And. . .

APRIL RUIZ is a sixth grade student at Sandburg Middle School.

SMALL TOWN, SMALL FOREST

● ● ● ● ● ● ● ● ● ● ● ● ● ●

SADIE YORK

Once upon a time, there was a small forest right next to a small town. Everybody said never to go in the forest or else you will never come out. One day, October 31, 1979, a group of teenagers decided to sneak out to the forest. In their friend group there were two girls, Kayla and Harper, and two boys, Jake and Kris. They all told their parents they were sleeping over at Kayla's house. When it hit 11 p.m., Kayla's parents came in and said good night, then they packed their stuff and left. They went on their bikes and headed to the forest. They got to the forest and they all got chills down their spine. The trees looked taller than ever and it was dark and cold and pretty scary. They set up a big tent because they were planning on spending the night there. They all went to sleep.

They were all asleep when Kayla got up and heard a baby cry. She got scared. She woke up Jake and he heard it too. They decided to go out and check it out. Kayla said, "I'm scared." Jake said, "Don't worry. It's probably nothing," then started walking back to the tent, but when he almost got to the tent he heard Kayla scream. Everybody got up and ran out of the tent. When everybody got out she was gone. There was no sign of her. Everybody was scared. Kris said, "We

should go look for her," with his voice breaking up. Harper replied, saying "Let's split up," so they all split up. Harper was walking around looking when all of a sudden she heard the crying too. She got super scared and thought maybe splitting up wasn't a good idea. That's when somebody from behind her grabbed her mouth so she couldn't scream, picked her up, and started running somewhere. Harper was fighting back so hard but they were just too strong. They threw her down into a room and Harper was bawling her eyes out. That's when she saw Kayla there too. They hugged right away and were both crying .

The boys met up and started to look for Harper and Jake said, "Let's go get the police. I'm scared." Kris said, "Yeah," while almost about to pee his pants. They headed over to the police station and told the police officer at the front desk, "Come to the forest. Two girls went missing there." They sent out two men with them and they found a door that led underground. They explored and found a room and heard two girls screaming very very loudly. The door was locked and the policemen kicked it down. The girls were so relieved and when the man heard that, he ran to the room. When the policemen saw him, they tackled him and arrested him.

Meanwhile, back at Kayla's house, her mom went to go check up on them and she realized they were gone. She was so furious she went to the police and on her way to the police station, she saw the police car by the forest and went to go check on what had happened. She saw her daughter Kayla, ran up to her, hugged her, and started crying. She said, "I was so worried," while Kayla was just bawling her eyes out into her mom's arms.

SADIE YORK is a sixth grade student at Sandburg Middle School.

THE CABIN

● ● ● ● ● ● ● ● ● ● ● ● ● ● ●

ETHAN BUCK

It was dark in the forest. I didn't know where I was. My phone had just died. I was hungry and thirsty but I couldn't find any food or water. It started to get dark and windy.

It was getting cold, and I was getting tired. So I needed to find my cabin fast. I found some berries but I didn't know if they were poisonous or not. It was so dark out that I could not see that far. After a little while, I found some food and water.

After that, I went back on my journey. I saw something.. I started to run very fast after it. I was running for a long time when I saw my cabin. I started to hide. I saw a person outside after he left, then I went to sleep. I woke up and ate some food. I went back to sleep in the afternoon and I saw my friend in the city. We were eating, then after I went home.

ETHAN BUCK is a sixth grade student at Sandburg Middle School. He likes to eat pizza for lunch and play basketball. On Sundays, Ethan plays video games with his friends, but first he eats pizza.

THE TREASURE IN THE MANSION

●━●━●━●━●━●━●━●━●━●━●━●━●━●━●

NOAH WURPTS

One spooky night in the creepy forest, Max felt a cold breeze. Then he saw a haunted mansion that chilled him to the bone. But then he saw treasure through a broken window. He stepped back thinking what to do.

Then he ran back, his feet stepping on the dead leaves. He made it out safely and went to his friend's house. They start talking about the mansion when there was a knock on the door. They froze thinking it was the rumored ghost of the mansion but it was the mailman. He told his friend about the treasure in the mansion. His friend asked what was it Max said, "I don't know."

"Okay, let's find out," said his friend. Then he replied, "Okay." They got there and a ghost was looking at the treasure. They slowly walked back. Then the ghost disappeared into the darkness.

They did not go home. They carefully walked to the gate. It opened with a creak. They saw a tree with a face that creeped them out. At the door the ghost was waiting. It seemed friendly so they approached it.

They asked for the treasure. The ghost revealed it was a picture of his family. When Max saw that, he and his friend

were disappointed. And it smelled like dirty socks. The ghost got mad and started to attack them, driving them off forever.

NOAH WURPTS is a sixth grade student at Sandburg Middle School. What he enjoys about writing is making up stories. His favorite sport is baseball

STILL ALIVE

● ● ● ● ● ● ● ● ● ● ● ● ● ● ●

AVA LUNDBERG

It was 11:00 p.m., as Mattow and Veronica slowly drove on the highway. They were heading to the Freinders Cave. Mattow sighed. "You said this place was scary, but tell me about it."

Veronica thought for a moment. "Well, people say it's haunted by creatures centuries old. Creatures with bodies that are made of diamond and stone, so the creatures could escape their bodies. They went insane, and now they're crazy killing machines. But, eh, I don't believe that. People have died there though, but only because of natural causes."

Mattow nodded, "Well we're here, so let's see if all this monster nonsense is true." Veronica nodded, and they both stepped out of the car. It was a small dirt parking lot, and there was a small staircase in the middle of it leading down to the cave. The staircase went down about a hundred steps, and by the time they reached the bottom, they were panting and struggling to breathe. They traveled down a long hallway and found themselves in a wide clearing with a big wooden desk in the middle.

A woman stood at the desk. She was wearing a smile. "Hello, are you two here for the horrors of the cave?" she asked.

They both nodded. "Nice, nice, nice. That will be fifty

dollars then, please and thank you!" Mattow took a check out of his pocket and gave it to her.

Then the two of them, Veronica and Mattow, walked into a large opening behind the desk. As they walked, they talked about how they couldn't believe any of the nonsense that others have said about the cave. Then they arrived upon five large openings that all led in different directions. They walked up to the fourth opening and then . . . the head of a dog shot out from the darkness. It was completely white and missing an eye. It was wearing a pink collar with a leash attached to it. The leash was made out of bones and it seemed to go on forever behind the dog Veronica flinched, and Mattow fell to the ground.

Then the creature started to scream at them, "I'm pretty right? RIGHT? AHHHHHHH! TELL ME I'M PRETTY! TELL ME NOW!" Neither of the two spoke a word, and then the dog lunged at Mattow. It dug its fangs in him and dragged him away.

Then from the darkness, Veronica heard the dog laugh. "IF I'M NOT PRETTY . . . THEN I MUST BE DEADLY!!! HA HA HA! THAT'S EVEN BETTER!!!" Then the dog swallowed Mattow, and Veronica sank to the ground in tears. Then the woman from the desk appeared behind her. "What happened? I heard you crying . . ."

Veronica sobbed, "T-the dog, the dog, the dog, the dog!!!"

The lady laughed. "No need to worry. The dog and all the other creatures here are fake. They're robots!"

Veronica shook her head and screamed, "IT KILLED HIM!! IT KILLED HIM! IT KILLED HIM!"

The lady sighed. "What are you talking about? There was never anyone with you."

AVA LUNDBERG lives in Golden Valley in a house at a dead end with her dad and stepmother. She participates in three sports, which are quadrobics, rock climbing,

and swimming. Ava finds it harder to write short stories instead of long ones. Ava also LOVES TATERTOTS.

THE DARK

TOMIJEA

One night in the cold me and some friends were in a park playing scary games. Then all of a sudden my friend Katie was missing. Me and my other friend Miyah started looking for her. We heard her and we started following the sound. But then she stopped. We called her name but there was no response. Then we suddenly see a tall, black figure chasing her down. We tried to go and stop it, but we couldn't. He ran right through us.

"It was like nothing was there," Miyah cried. "Hey it's okay, we will find Katie, okay? Just follow me to the shed and let's grab some stuff to trap the monster," I said. We headed to the shed where we found stuff like a shovel, bear traps. We stuffed our backpacks full of stuff we think could stop the monster. Then we saw our friend running, but we didn't see the monster.

"HELP! MIYAH AND ERICA PLEASE HELP! ME THAT THING IS COMING! IT HAD A NOTE AND I GRABBED IT, HERE!" she tossed the note to me. I read it out loud.

The note said, "This monster can only be stopped by getting a shovel and a leaf blower and some gas from a car. Make sure someone is with the monster or he will get out. You guys, right now, whoever is reading this, get out of there quickly. I wrote this note because I made the monster but he

got out my lab so quick. Bring him back to my lab. Here's the address: 6345 Franklin Street South. Now you guys better hurry. Sincerely, Anonymous."

"OH NO!" I shouted, "We need a leaf blower. But we have no money." We headed to the store to go find a leaf blower. We walked in and asked the cashier if she has money that we can use.

"How old are you guys? And what for?" she asked.

"We need a leaf blower for a mon– sorry. My father needs one for his job and he's out finding one right now. But he needs our help. Is it possible you guys have one?" I said.

"G-g-go ahead children there's one at the back, okay."

We headed to the back of the store and found a leaf blower and we took it. We went and looked for Katie, but she was already gone so we tried to find the monster. We saw the monster and he was sleeping, so we looked at each other and we headed over to the monster. We turned on the leaf blower and we sucked up the monster. Then we rollerbladed to the lab. We looked at it and we put the leaf blower down and we put a note on it for the creator. We left for our houses and we got a phone call from the lab.

I answered and he said, "Thank you for the note and the leaf blower. The monster is safe and sound. I won't turn him on and play with him ever again."

I asked him, "What's the shovel for though?"

"It's for nothing. . ." he said. We hung up and the next day I met with my friend and we found Katie terrified and we said it was okay, the monster was not here anymore. She said, "Good!" We hugged each other and we laughed.

TOMIJEA IS a sixth grade student at Sandburg Middle School.

CAMP MOONLIGHT MERGE

PARKER ELLISON

It was the final day of middle school. So on the last day of school, we were all talking about what we were going to do during summer.

"I'm finally going to attempt to ride the big ramp at the skatepark!" Troy said with amazement in his eyes. The history of that ramp was big. Tony Hawk rode that ramp.

"I'm just spending mine at my gran's." Rose said. "

Really? Like, your regular grandma, or the one with all the candy?" Alex asked.

"The one with the candy." she replied.

"OMG! Can you bring some back with you?!?" everyone asked. She nodded her head. Then it was my turn.

"Come on Pete, whatcha doin' for summer?" Alex bugged me.

"I'm going to summer camp." I said, my face red and hot with embarrassment.

"Yeah, you know, I'm not going to ride the ramp. Or even skate AT ALL this summer. My folks are also sending me to camp." Troy said.

"What camp are they expelling you guys to?" Rose asked.

"Camp MoonLight Merge, why?" I asked.

"Do you guys not know the legends of that camp?" Alex asked.

"What legends?" I asked Alex back.

"Nevermind, let's just celebrate the last day of middle school with positive vibes! Okay?"Rose said. And we walked out of school feeling like high schoolers.

That night, I was so busy thinking about camp, and what Alex had said about the legends, I didn't eat my dinner.

"Are you okay, Petey?" Mom asked.

"I'm fine, just not as hungry as usual." I replied.

"Okay, just go upstairs and get some rest. Because we're driving you to camp tomorrow morning."

I just sighed a sigh that meant I hate life. I opened my door and walked straight to my phone mesmerized by it. Two missed calls and twelve new messages. My calls were just Troy. Probably wanting to talk about camp. I look at the texts and half are from my friends, while the rest are from the camp. "Welcome to your new favorite place to be!!!" it said. More like "welcome to your new place in hell." I texted Troy to ask if he got the same texts. I walked over to my computer and typed in MoonLight Merge. Nothing. I hit the refresh button. Still nothing. Whatever my computer is like, nine years old. It doesn't quite work. I went to my phone to Google it. Same response. Nothing. But my phone is one month old.

"Hey, Mom? What's that camp you're sending me to?" I yelled downstairs.

"MoonLight Merge. Why?"

"Where did you find out about it?" I asked.

"On the internet. Why?" she replied. I told her about my failed google search about the camp. "Well, that camp is pretty old. Been around since my time." she said. "You know, ancient times." she added in a mocking voice.

"Okay, okay. I just wanted to know if it still existed. That's all."

I went back upstairs to my room. It doesn't make sense. A camp as old as my mom, not on the internet. I thought I was just tired so I went to sleep. My dream was weird. I must've been at camp because of the cabins and the docks. But the cabins had moss growing at a speed that defied nature. And the docks looked splintered and broken. I heard sounds that would leave anyone looking pale. I looked around and saw Troy running toward me, arms flailing.

"We have to run!" he said, panting. "We have to get away from the camp."

"Why?" I was scared. I looked at where Troy was standing, but all I could see was a body on the ground. Not moving. I tried to scream, but no sound came out. I saw what looked like a counselor, aiming a firework at me. I couldn't run, I couldn't move. And then I couldn't live.

I woke up, drenched in cold sweat. I began my normal routine, pretending like nothing happened in my dream. I got dressed and when I looked in the mirror, I could've sworn I saw a ghost behind me. I shook my head, then looked back in the mirror. Nothing.

"Pete! We're going to be late if you don't hurry!" Mom yelled. In the car I looked back through the rear window. At one point I swore I saw the counselor from my dream. He propped up his firework and lit it. I blinked and in that duration of time, he was gone. When we got to the camp, I saw people setting up fireworks. My heart started to race. Then it picked up speed when the same EXACT counselor greeted me and my family. I looked around and saw Troy and ran over to him.

"Bro, I have a very bad feeling about this camp," we said in sync. We walked over to one of the port-a-potties and started talking.

"I had a dream about this place." I said.

"Lemme guess, fireworks, mossy cabins, broken docks, me dead?" He described my dream right that second.

"Did you have it too?" I asked. "Yeah, except you were dead first."

"Huh. Look, we need a plan that doesn't lead us to dying–"

"Well here ya are, now say goodbye to yer' youngins', adults," the counselor said.

The parents yelled bye at the same time. We walked over to the cabins and put our stuff away. After every cringey camp song, show, and food, it was time for the fireworks. I felt someone brush my shoulder, I whipped around to see two kids on a swing set looking at me weird.

"Run!" I heard Troy yell.

"I figured out why this camp is so weird. So I was hungry, as usual, so I went to raid the fridge. And what I saw was hu-" he stopped mid-sentence.

"Troy, what's in the counselor's fridge?" I asked, my voice full of concern. The kids appeared behind me again, with happiness on their faces.

"Do you know what happened?" I asked.

I looked back at where Troy was standing and instead of standing up he was laying on the floor with a firework in his back. I looked up and saw the counselor load up another firework, aimed it at me, and the countdown began.

Ten. I looked at the kids, but I couldn't find them. Nine. The swingset too. Eight. I tried to run as far as I could in different directions. Seven. But the counselor united and had the camp circled. Six. I tried to run into the camp, but the counselor caught me. Five. I'm lying in front of all these counselors and campers, defenseless. Four. "Well as you have learned from yer buddy back there," the counselor yelled to all the campers. Three. "is to not go tellin' secrets to other campers." He spat in my face. Two. "Cus' then they end up in the fridge! Hahaha!" The escape of my death was not possible. I accepted what I had lived to be. And that I was going

to die, right here. Right now. One. I couldn't run, I couldn't move. Zero. I couldn't breathe.

PARKER ELLISON is a sixth grade student at Sandburg Middle School. Parker lives in New Hope, Minn., with his mom, dad, and two siblings. Parker identifies as gender fluid and bisexual.

THE DARK FIGURE

OWEN DRAPER

Owen, Olivia, and Bentley were walking to their houses after school and they decided to not go home and instead explore this forest where people say there are ghosts. Bentley was scared. They walked across the street and went into the forest. They were in there for maybe an hour until the sun went down and they instantly felt as if someone was watching them all the time. Bentley was making Owen and Olivia walk on both sides of her.

The three of them heard ominous noises they have never heard before. The grass was moist from last night's rain, they could hear the sound of water dripping off of leaves. Bentley kept on saying, "Please can we just go home? My mom is gonna be so mad at me." But Owen and Olivia didn't care. The moon was especially dim that night, so they could barely see what was in front of them. Owls were hooting, squirrels were running around and there were all sorts of bugs. Bentley, Owen, and Olivia still felt like they were being watched. They felt a sudden gust of wind and it got colder. Owen and Olivia were deciding if they should listen to Bentley and go back home, but they decided they have already spent a long time in this forest. Why back out now? They saw a floating white pair of antlers run across the forest. Bentley screamed at the top of her lungs and they saw the white pair of antlers turn around to reveal two glowing white eyes.

They all looked at each other but Olivia was gone. Bentley and Owen looked back at the monster and it was gone too, they both started sprinting and Owen had looked back and Bentley had tripped on the roots of a tree. While he was looking at her she disappeared in a split second. Owen kept on running away and suddenly there was a shadowy black figure that looked like a moose on its hind legs with glowing white eyes and antlers. The figure zipped away and was never seen by Owen again.

OWEN DRAPER is a sixth grade student at Sandburg Middle School. He doesn't like to write, but he will when he has to. Owen plays football and wants to own a restaurant with his brother

SCIENCE FICTION AND FANTASY STORIES

THE SAD, EVENTFUL, AND DRAMATIC LIFE OF IRIS

- - - - - - - - - - - - - - -

Evelyn Mullenmaster

The day I met my best friend, Tahis, was also the worst day of my life. And keep in mind, I was just four. I woke up and I heard crying, so I got up to find out what happened. It was my mom. My mom rented the house we lived in, and she threw my dad out because he didn't help raise me or pay for anything. Let's just say my dad was NOT happy about that, so he stole all of our valuables and money. But he died later that day in a street fight. Later that day, the landlord came and evicted us because my mom wasn't paying the bills. Now she couldn't, because my dad took all we had. He had spent all the money already, though we were not sure what for. We were stuck on the streets. A little while after that, we went to the park. My mom told me that we were going to live at the park for a while. I didn't care because all I thought that meant was that we were going to play every day. Even though he didn't help take care of me, I really wish my mom didn't throw out my dad. I missed him. A little while later, I saw another girl my age at the park and she asked if I wanted to play. I said "Yes, of course!" We went on

everything at the park. She told me about her dad and I told her about my mom. We realized we had a lot in common, so I asked if she wanted to be friends. She said yes! I was so glad that I had someone to talk to that wasn't my mom. Don't get me wrong, I loved my mom. It's just that I liked talking to my friends more. For example, if I had to talk about my mom, I would talk to my friends. But before that I had none, so I'm thankful that I had one now. And to top it all off, my mom took me to work with her later that day because she had nowhere for me to go. She got fired because of that. At that point she just gave up. I would have given up too. I would have to care for myself and her forever, unless I wanted both of us to die. And I couldn't watch another parent go. I could barely watch my dad go. Even though he didn't care, I still loved him.

But one day, my mom met Tahis's dad and they instantly fell in love. When I say that they fell in love, I mean that they were practically made for eachother. (That day was one of the best days of my life.) They got married with money my new dad stole from a bank. I was glad my mom was finally living the life she deserved. Before I knew it, I had a half–baby brother named Liam. I knew I had to protect him. My mom and Tahis were getting along better than ever. Even if my stepdad wasn't the best role model, I was thankful to have a father figure. We also moved into an apartment with the leftover money from the wedding. The only bad part about that apartment was that Tahis, Liam, and I all had to share a room. It wasn't a very big apartment, but it was better than living at the park. For the time being, I was living the dream compared to my old life. We lived happily ever after in our new life. Just kidding, I wish that happened. Our parents died in a car accident. Since we were only seven and Liam, our little brother, was two, we became orphans. Eventually we all got adopted into the same family. They didn't have any other kids; it was just us. On Tahis's and my 18th birthday, our adopted parent kicked us and Liam out. They told us

that we were old enough to take care of Liam and live on our own. And we did take care of Liam until he married. My brother, Liam, married a rich lady named Lacey at just nineteen. And my sister and I moved into a one-room apartment together at twenty. Before we moved into an apartment and Liam married, we lived in a homeless shelter because we couldn't afford anything better. But Tahis and I thankfully had jobs to pay for food and stuff. We were only cashiers at a gas station, so it didn't pay very well, but we got fired from our job because we were stealing money and food. Since our childhoods were so bad, we decided to get revenge on the world. We changed our names to Flower and Floral, but we go by Dahlia and Iris. She was my sister sidekick, and I was thankful to have her. Our duo name was The Red Roses. Of course, we did a lot of bad things—yes, including crime—but we had to do something to top it all off. But the question was, what would we do?

Dahlia and I were thirty-nine, and Liam was thirty-four. On my brother's oldest son, Liam Jr.'s, fifteenth birthday, my brother died. His wife killed him because he didn't pay any bills or help raise their five kids. (Liam reminded me of my dad, which wasn't a good thing to be reminded of, but still, he was my little brother. I had got to stick up for him, which meant I couldn't let this happen.) I had to protect him and I failed. I let him die. But she got away with it by bribing the cop. I'm not sure how much she bribed them with, but it was probably a lot. But Dahlia and I weren't going to let her get away with that. We made it our mission to kill her. We snuck in the house at exactly midnight. We didn't have any plan. I guess our plan was just to go with the flow. But we had to be sneaky about it because this was our biggest challenge yet. Lacey had very high tech security and lived in a gated community.

The day of the revenge, I was scared yet so excited.. We slowly and carefully climbed over the gate. Thankfully, we didn't get caught. We made our way to their house by

going through the front door. We used the key our brother gave us before he died. We slowly, carefully made our way up the stairs. But when we got upstairs, the lasers went on. Thankfully we made it through without setting any alarms off. But when we got to Lacey's room, there were a series of traps. Thankfully it wasn't anything we hadn't seen before, so we made it through. But Lacey woke up and had a gun that she tried to shoot us with. But thankfully she failed and ran out of bullets. At the speed of light, Dahlia killed her with a sword we stole from a museum. Then we dashed out by jumping out the window. It was only one story high and we had done this many times before. But sadly I hit the side of the house and died. And that was the end of my life. I'm not sure what happened after that. I hope Dahlia survived. But at least I died knowing that I got to make those kids suffer like Dahlia, Liam, and I did.

Author's Note:

If you liked this story, make sure to take a look at Genesis Escoto Sotelo's version of the story The Sad, Eventful, and Dramatic Life Of Dahlia. It is an amazing story where she writes from Dahlia's point of view. It also tells you about her home life before she met Iris, what happened to her mom, what happened to Dahlia after Iris died, and life before she entered her new life. Genesis is a very good friend of mine. And fun fact, Dahlia's name before she changed her name (Tahis) is actually Genesis's middle name in real life.

EVELYN MULLENMASTER is a sixth grader at Sandburg Middle School. She lives with her mom, dad, and annoying sister. If she could spend a Saturday with anyone doing anything, it would be with her four besties at the mall. Evelyn is a Red Cross Certified

babysitter. Her favorite color is pastel purple. She has also been a vegetarian for around five years.

THE SAD, EVENTFUL, AND DRAMATIC LIFE OF DAHLIA

• ● ● ● ● ● ● ● ● ● ● ● ● ● ●

GENESIS ESCOTO SOTELO

I was four years old when I learned that not everyone in society was quite equal. I was only four, but I had to take care of myself. My mom died when I was born, and my father gave up on life after her death. I had to find food to feed myself and survive. Even when we had no money, the only thing that made me feel alive was reading and drawing. One day I was walking to the park when I saw a girl my age. She looked kinda sad, so I asked her if she wanted to play with me. We started talking. She told me about her mom and her, and I told her about my dad. That's how we realized that we had a lot in common. She asked me if we could be friends. Of course I said yes. From then on, we would see each other at the park every day.

One day, my dad and her mom met each other and instantly fell in love. A few months later, my father stole from a bank to buy the things for the wedding. Soon after, I had a half brother, and with the leftover money we moved into an apartment. My friend, Beata and my father got along pretty well. I was glad that dad was finally happy, and I was happy

to have a mom that loved me. I thought we were finally going to have a happy life, but we didn't. About two years after our parents got married, they sadly died in a car accident. We were only seven, and Liam was only two years old. We became orphans.

After a bit of time, we got adopted into the same family. The years passed by and we grew up. Liam married a rich lady named Lacey at nineteen. In the past, our parents had kicked us out when we turned eighteen, so Iris and I had to find a way to take care of Liam. We had told him that when he was old enough, he had to marry someone rich.We changed names to Flower and Floral, but we went by Dahlia and Iris. Iris had decided to get revenge on the world for not helping us when needed, and of course I was going to help her. After all, she was my sister. I was her sidekick. Our duo name was The Red Roses. In the past we did bad things, but we were planning on doing something very bad. You could say it was the cherry on the top.

On our brother's son's fifteenth birthday, our brother was killed. We knew who did it. Liam was not a good father, but we knew that. The person who killed Liam was Lacey, his wife. She did it because we knew that the person who hated Liam the most was Lacey. After we found out that the cops were not going to do anything about Liam's death, Iris and I decided that we were going to kill Lacey. We made it our mission. We were going to sneak into her house at exactly midnight. Iris didn't have a plan. But she said to go with the flow. And we would have to be sneaky about it, because it was one of the biggest crimes yet. Lacey also had very advanced tech.

Iris was very upset about Liam's death and very mad that she was not able to protect Liam. I was also mad at Liam's death, but I had to be strong for Iris. The day we were planning to sneak into Lacey's house, I was not surprised to see Iris quite excited yet scared. We were able to enter the property quite easily. We made it in without getting caught. We luckily had a pair of keys Liam had given us. The house was full

of lasers. Of course we studied where each laser was, so that when we went into the house, we didn't set off any alarms. I was prepared for anything that could come at us. Then I realized that Lacey had woken up and tried to set off an alarm that would tell the cops what was going on. But thankfully, Iris blocked it while I ran as fast as I could and killed Lacey with a sword that we stole from a museum. Right as I killed her, I jumped out the window. I didn't get hurt because it was only one story high. Plus we had done this before, so it was not a problem. I thought everything was fine, but when I looked beside me, Iris was dead. I had nobody in this world to call family; they were all dead. I didn't know what to do, but the first thing I did was get Iris's body and run away.

Days after Iris's death, I buried Iris beside Liam's grave. I had no reason to go on with life, so I went to Liam's, Iris's, and what is now my grave, and I buried myself. At least I was going to be with my family. That was the end of me.

Author's Note:
If you would like to read from Iris's perspective, look for the story of Evelyn Mullenmaster. Fun fact: Evelyn's middle name is her character's name before she changed it (Beata). She is a close friend of mine. Thank you for reading this.

GENESIS ESCOTO SOTELO is a sixth grade student at Sandburg Middle School. She lives in Minneapolis.

JADE 428

● ● ● ● ● ● ● ● ● ● ● ● ●

JULIANA ANDERSON

Okay... Answer my question, what's worse: running from guards or running from a blown up lab you destroyed? I can't choose! They are both happening to me at the moment. Well it's nice to meet you. I'm Experiment 428, or Jade. I'm a mutated human and I have "godlike" power. The lab made me who I am today! And I absolutely regret my choice. Then again I don't. The lab fused me with a Canadian Marble Fox and electricity into my blood. Quite shocking that is. Breathe in, breathe out. I'm hiding behind a tree at the moment. Noises of buzzing flashing lights go past. "Well, the rest got five seconds to live," I mumble. I dash past the floating hoverbikes. No one notices me, I'm just a blur in their sight. Three, two, one... A loud burst goes off behind me. I don't look or even acknowledge what I did, no one will notice. I bet the army will though. Their weapon in training is never coming back. EVER.

I grasp my swords, the noise of buzzing fills the air again. Lights flash in every direction, soon landing on me. "We found her," one says, "Don't move or else you know what will happen." Their stares creep up my back. My expression is blank, but deep down I'm lost. My eyes flash red, warning them to not come any closer. My eyes darted from left to right. I either run for it or I let them take control of me, again. Decisions, decisions, hmm... Neither! My eyes flash

faster, footsteps shuffle, and I tense. Soon they are less than three meters in front of me, at this point my eyes have finished flashing red, warning red soon turned into deadly red. My grip tightens, every single one of their movements counts. I glance around the area. There are at least twenty guards and machines pointed at me. I grimace. Great, they made themselves obvious. Just like that, silence. My motions are swift and fast, no sound, just the cool crisp air.

I regret it, but I don't! I'd still be in the crappy lab, which had the weirdest stench. It smelled like something died, then was becoming moldy. Yeah. . . It was disgusting. I was sent there when I was five due to my father having to escape something. I don't really remember, but all I know is that he loved me and I loved him! My town was attacked and bombed way back when. I was the only survivor of my family, and townspeople. I was only two. But I somehow remember it. It's like when you remember something traumatic and then forget everything else, if that's ever happened to you. I don't remember much of the years before it, just a man who rescued me, he always looked at me with soft caring eyes. Father, hmm.. I wonder if he's doing okay. I miss him, more than anything, but FINALLY I can reunite with him and life will turn out perfectly, yay! That's a lie, lying inside of itself. Well, the good part is I'm free, that's until the military finds me, and I'll be sent to another training facility. Once I get there, they'll probably all kill me. They killed the old me, the present me won't be taken away. Ever, never again will they take me down.

JULIANA ANDERSON is a sixth grade student at Sandburg Middle School. Juliana loves to draw! Art has always been something she loves to do forever! Juliana plays softball in the summer and ice skates in the winter. Things she likes include art, anime, animals, nature and sushi.

UNKNOWN TO EARTH

● ● ● ● ● ● ● ● ● ● ● ● ● ● ●

ROBYN

A x woke up on the street not knowing what happened the night before. He tried his best to think of what happened. He couldn't remember it that clearly because he was hit on the head.

"Ow, my entire body hurts so much," He muttered. "Wait, I think I remember a little bit from last night. . ."

"We have to!"
"He's going to die!" Ax's mother said from the kitchen.
"Okay. . ." Ax's dad said sadly.
"Ax, can you come here please?" Ax walked into the kitchen but only saw his mom even though he knew he heard his dad. Before he could say anything, all he could see. . . was black.

Now he was on a street he was not familiar with. He looked everywhere but couldn't see a single building he recognized; they all looked so weird. He looked around and saw people avoiding him and even some running away.

"DON'T GO NEAR THAT MONSTER!"

"STAY AWAY FROM HIM!"

"What. . . happened?"

Suddenly he saw a fork fly towards him. He put up his hand so it didn't hit his face. But instead of it hitting his hand it fell on the ground, covered in ice.

"What. . ?" he said under his breath.

"FREAK!"

"NO WONDER HE HAS DEVIL HORNS AND ELF EARS. HE'S A MONSTER!" Ax realized that no one looked like him.

"Where. . . am I?" Ax said. "Wait a second, you are. . .humans!" Ax realized. "HOW DID I GET HERE!" Ax looked around. Everyone was staring at him just as confused as he was. Ax didn't know what else to do. So he ran away. He decided he would live the rest of his life running from the police, training, and becoming stronger.

Ax is 13 now. It had been three years since he was dumped on earth. People were still calling him a freak and a monster. The police had been after him since he appeared on Earth.

Ax heard sirens. "Already? They think that trying to catch me at five in the morning will work? They realize I'm not a human right? I don't sleep." Ax said to himself. Ax started running. The police cars chased after him.

"STOP RIGHT THERE!" a policeman yelled loud enough that Ax was sure he would wake up the entire town.

"Good luck catching me," Ax said, running faster. Ax quickly formed an ice wall. The cars immediately stopped. As the policemen were getting out of the cars, Ax started blasting icicles at them, forcing them to take cover and get back into the cars. Ax ran into an alleyway.

"Well, that was fun." Ax said, satisfied. Maybe his parents put him on Earth to become stronger. *BAM!* Ax heard a loud crash behind him. He spun around. It was a baby alien. Had she been dumped on Earth by her parents too? He decided to take her in.

"I won't let her be called a freak like me."

ROBYN IS a sixth grade student at Sandburg Middle School. She lives in Golden Valley with her parents, and six pets. Robyn's favorite sport is basketball and

she has been playing basketball since third grade. Robyn's favorite way to spend a Saturday is to hangout with her best friend!

SECRET ALIEN BASE

● ● ● ● ● ● ● ● ● ● ● ● ● ● ●

Mazen Elsaid

I was just chilling until my best friend woke me up. Zzarff said, "COME HERE RIGHT NOW!"

I said, "Why?"

He said, "JUST COME RIGHT NOW!"

"Ok fine," I said.

"They found a secret alien base."

"Should we check it out?"

"I don't know, should we?"

We went to check what was inside and we were surprised.

"OH MY GOD THERE IS SO MUCH DANGEROUS TECHNOLOGY," said Zzarff.

"WOW this is so cool," I said.

"Oh noooo, shhhh be quiet the aliens are sleeping. If we get caught we might get injured or 99 percent die," said Zzarff.

"Uhhhh okay?" I said. We got the lasers and snuck outside. "Are you sure we shouldn't put their dangerous technologies away?"

We felt this big breeze of chilly air.

"OMG A UFO," I said. "I TOLD YOU, WE SHOULD HAVE PUT THEIR STUFF BACK, IDIOT! OH MY GOD WE ARE GONNA DIE!!!"

"We have come to get our weapons back," said the aliens. (Oh, they are actually nice.)

"Here, take them back. We just wanted to see them," Zzarff and I said.

"Okay." The aliens took the weapons and left.

MAZEN ELSAID is a sixth grade student at Sandburg Middle School.

BLOB MANIA

• ● ● ● ● ● ● ● ● ● ● ● ● ● ● ●

DREA LIND

Once upon a time, in a land far, far away—well, not so far for you, but for this particular girl it was—the land was. . . EARTH. The girl's name was Bondeshia, and Bondeshia was the last human on Earth. She thought she last saw humans when she was fourteen and was stuck in a time warp for two years. Now she was sixteen and could drive. Her main goal was to find another human before she died. One of her greatest fears was turning into a blob like all the other blobs on Earth.

So one day, she set out and wanted to see if she could find another human. After all, that was her lifelong goal. So she found a car in an alley, and it was so beat up that it had rust all over the doors. She tried to get in, but on her first try she failed because the doors were so stuck with the rust. Eventually she made it in the car and off she was on her journey! She was kinda doubtful that she would find anyone, but she decided to push away all of those thoughts and keep going. She finally remembered that she couldn't be seen by the other blobs, or else they would take her away and turn her into one of them. She was very scared, and that made it that much harder. But she had a plan. . . There were secret alleys where nobody would see her, and she could get away from the area she was in.

So she was about halfway to where she thought there was

another human. She spotted a blob just chillin' outside her window, and she screamed in terror. She tried to close her eyes, thinking it was a dream, but it wasn't. . . She then realized that maybe she should try to talk to the blob, so she did. She had a lump in her throat and her stomach felt like it had a knot in it.

"Hi," she said.

"Umm, hi?" the blob said back.

"So what's your name?" she said.

"Um, my name is Wubble. What's yours?" the blob responded.

"My name is Bondeshia," she responded. And then she invited Wubble into her car, and she ended up actually liking the blob.

They had a lot of fun together. They played games together, like tic-tac-toe and Sorry, and ate together. They ended up staying together for a while, and she was wondering why she was getting along with this blob so well and he wasn't making her into one of them. So she asked him, and he responded that he just got turned into a human seconds before they met. She realized that this blob was the other human she was searching for! When she found that out, she realized that she didn't have to do any more searching and could just live with this blob. So that's exactly what they did; they lived together for the rest of her life, in her car.

DREA LIND is a sixth grader at Sandburg Middle School. She lives in New Hope, Minn.

COLD

● ● ● ● ● ● ● ● ● ● ● ● ● ● ●

FRANK

So he woke up on Planet A, where he saw that he did not look like the others. When he tried to speak to them, he turned into them. But they only looked at him. He recognized that they had pupils and he did not.

Then out of nowhere, a weird spaceship popped up. The beings on the spaceship looked like robot versions of the ones from Planet A. Then they teleported him into a cell where they said he would be killed. He ate his way through them, and he made it into a spaceship where he went into space. He was shot down by a beam, and it started pulling the spaceship back. Then he got out of it. He floated into space, to the last planet.

Then he landed the spaceship on the golden planet, where there were some goo people like him. He tried to eat them but he could not. He started turning gold-ish, and then turned into a solid form. It cracked, which spilled more goo. The goo was sent back to his home planet by the goo robots. The home planet was now fully gone, so they sent the goo into a museum. He was stuck there for the rest of his life. . . until the robot planet got destroyed by the gold one.

Both planets crashed into each other, then he was freed. Now he floated onto the red planet. He turned into a red one and made himself some pupils with some goo of his that

he spilled. Then he lived his infinite life being something he was not.

FRANK LIKES games, food, and hates super loud noises. He likes to play a little bit of soccer and he wants to be a lawyer when he grows up.

SCARLET EYE

● ● ● ● ● ● ● ● ● ● ● ● ● ● ● ●

NATASHA DUTTON

S he feels blind as the darkness coats her eyes. The sharp blade is gripped by her soft hands. The blade is coated in a warm, red liquid, and the feeling of defeat sinks down in the young assassin's stomach. The scarlet's eyes open, and she comes out of hiding after quickly completing her job. She thinks to herself, *More people died this time. Dang it* . . . She quickly hops out the shattered window, landing gracefully.

Now she's on her own, walking on the concrete. Luckily, her formal disguise is mostly black and red. The blade is hidden behind a sheet of her clothing and shielded from the outside world. A certain shard of something catches the scarlet eye. The girl assumes that it is just a fragment of the shattered window she sprung out of. "What the–" The shard isn't an ordinary slice of glass. It has these strange markings on it, almost like it was from hundreds of years ago.

What's with these awkward lines? the girl thinks to herself and lifts the piece off of the ground. It is textured, and the feeling of the dry shard rubs against the soft skin of the girl. The fragment glistens in the moonlight. It sparkles more than usual, and the girl begins to slowly lose her consciousness. The shard slips from her hands and shatters to tiny pieces.

Days, hours, minutes. It feels like forever before the girl comes to her senses. It is almost like she is in an old play.

There aren't any phone booths, and everyone looks like they are from hundreds of years ago.

NATASHA DUTTON is a sixth grade student at Sandburg Middle School.

THE SEARCH

• ● ● ● ● ● ● ● ● ● ● ● ● ●

DRE JOHNSTON

Phil was searching for his friend Steven. He had been asking around his town for him, and even asked Steven's parents. They had no sign of him either. Phil got an email from an unknown person. Phil found it strange but he still decided to read it. The email read, "If you ever want to see your friend again come to the forest twenty miles out of your town." Phil felt chills go down his neck. He thought about whether he should go and get help or just go by himself. He decided to go by himself because he thought about how no one would believe him. Phil got in his car and started to head to the forest. He finally reached the forest. He got out of his car and opened the trunk of the car and took out a flashlight, pocket knife, jacket, and a lockpick and started heading into the forest.

It was almost completely dark once Phil got a little deeper in the forest. He started to look for clues of his friend but he saw no trace of him. Still, he kept heading further and further into the forest. He looked at his phone to see what battery it was at and it was getting low. A little bit of sweat beaded down his forehead. Then he saw the bush to his left move. He pulled out his pocket knife from his back pocket and backed up. The bush made more and more sound. Then a small squirrel crawled out of the bush. Phil let out a big sigh

and put the pocket knife back in his back pocket and continued searching for his friend.

It was now pitch black outside and Phil could barely see anything, even with his flashlight. He kept thinking about just going back to his car and going back into town, but Phil was still thinking about Steven and if he was okay. Phil finally came across a cabin. He started to dash to the cabin as fast as he could. Phil started knocking on the door and nobody answered so he knocked again, and a little louder, and still there was no answer. So Phil started to look through the windows of the cabin and saw that nobody was there. Phil pulled out the lockpick he brought with him and started to use it on the door. Slowly, Phil opened the door and as soon as he stepped foot in the cabin the battery on the flashlight stopped working. He pulled out his phone to use the last of the battery. Looking around the small cabin, there was only one room and a very cramped living room. Phil tried looking for about thirty minutes. Phil's phone just reached one percent. He was losing hope of finding Steven, then he looked at the bear rug and saw a hatch and moved the rug out of the way. Phil pulled the hatch open slowly and climbed down into it.

Phil dropped down from the ladder and started to look around. He zipped up his jacket and rubbed his hands together and then started walking slowly around the dark room and heard a small cough.

"Hello!" Phil yelled. There was no response. Phil tried to locate where the cough came from and then all of a sudden the light cut out as Phil's phone died. Phil started walking again a little slower this time.

"Help," a small and raspy voice said.

"STEVEN, IS THAT YOU?" Phil said.

"Phil?" the voice said.

Phil started running to the voice. Phil finally found Steven. He was bruised and skinny but he was alive. Phil brought him back home and stayed with him for a while. To

this day Phil doesn't know who took Steven or who emailed him but Phil is glad he found his friend.

DRE JOHNSTON is a sixth grade student at Sandburg Middle School.

VLASK THE OCTOPUS

SCARLETT VANG

Deep down in the ocean there is an octopus named Vlask. He is an evil octopus and people never really knew why, but all Vlask is trying to do is get revenge. Vlask's dad passed away when Vlask was a baby, so now Vlask is trying to flood the earth so the human population will disappear. But Vlask never really knew what happened to his dad.

Vlask is on an adventure to go find out if his dad is actually dead or if the humans captured his dad. Little does he know, something is after him. While Vlask is doing his daily sinking of ships he sees something that looks familiar. It's something that belonged to Vlask's dad! It's Vlask's dad's unique bracelet he would wear all the time. Vlask thinks that his dad must be near so he searches and searches, but little does he know something is after him. Will he find his dad? What's after him? All that he knows is his dad is not safe.

SCARLETT VANG is a sixth grade student at Sandburg Middle School.

DEATH CITY

● ● ● ● ● ● ● ● ● ● ● ● ● ●

COLBY HOVDE

So the main character is a blonde haired, blue eyed guy named Justin and he has two helpers that help him rob and be bad and make bad decisions and right now Justin and his two helpers are in a twenty-four hour gas station in southern des moines, iowa and it is a clear night with a low fog. On a sunday evening, they are at the gas station specifically to go to the bathroom and get four sus items: cheetos, a hammer, saw, and a roll of garbage bags. Their transportation is three stolen bikes and they are planning to bike through the night forty miles to a southern town in Iowa called Death City. So they are about to bike to Death City when a cop car pulls into the gas station. The cops are at the gas station to get doughnuts because that's what cops do. But they come over to the three dudes and say, "Where are you off to?" And the dudes say they were at a party and now they're going to their houses, but little do the cops know they are actually going to Death City, Iowa.

After the cops left, Justin and his helpers were about to leave the gas station and Justin thinks the coast is clear but the cops are in the back alley ready to follow. Then a shooting star appears for 2.6 seconds and there are screams in the distance, but Justin doesn't care so the three dudes are off on their bikes towards Death City. Then the cops follow them

with their lights off. It is dark, so the three dudes still don't know the cops are following.

A little bit later it starts to rain and the three dudes are soaked and sweaty and gross. It just sucks and the cops are still following the three dudes. The sun starts to come up and they're about two miles from the farm in Death City and the rain goes away and it becomes foggy. The cops pull away and hide in the woods and the three dudes make it to the farm and there are two sets of french doors and the barn is painted blood red.

And there is a gray pond across the gravel street and the three dudes go and check it out and there are a lot of bodies, out cold. They call 911, and they say help is their way there, so the dudes are waiting for a while then finally the cops get to the pond three hours later. The cops are the same people and the gas station the previous night in Des Moines.

The cops say they know nothing about the bodies, and little did the dudes know the cops are the real villains.

To be continued...

COLBY HOVDE is a sixth grade student at Sandburg Middle School. Baseball is his favorite sport. Colby plays for Golden Valley Little League. He wants to be an umpire when he's old enough and play varsity baseball in high school. He also has a dog named Jet who loves to swim and chase tennis balls.

SHUT UP THE ROBOT

●   ●   ●   ●   ●   ●   ●   ●   ●   ●   ●   ●   ●   ●   ●

SHAYLA JOHNSON

Shut Up is a robot who wants to kill every human. He was made to help humans, but they were mean to him. He was angry so he put everyone in the city to sleep. He moved on to the next city and that was when he found a random person on the toilet with a soft object. It was warm and had a picture of an anime character named Yor Forger. Inside of the toilet there was a sword. He grabbed it and it was wet but he dried it off. The robot called it the donut sword because it reminded him of something he saw of a guy who had flames with the same sword. He had a hole in the middle of him and died. He put the guy with the sword to sleep and then he went on to put more people to sleep. Then he committed arson to an apartment building.

He found a large building and he made it his home. Inside, he found a small dog named Cheems. Cheems was a Shiba Inu and was very small. He also wore Adidas. Next, he went to a store and found a Rock Lee body pillow and he put it next to his Yor Forger pillow. Next, he went to Domino's and put all the workers to sleep. He saw a pizza cooking in the oven. He gave it to his dog to eat and the dog liked it. Soon enough, the police from the next town over came to kill him so he obviously wanted to attack them. Next, he decided to make a weapon to only hurt humans and not anything else. He went to the White House and launched the weapon. The

weapon worked, and it only put humans to sleep. Then, he found every dog in the world and adopted them. Now he had a dog army. Then, he saw something in the sky. It was an alien spaceship. He was planning on going up there next.

SHAYLA JOHNSON is a sixth grade student at Sandburg Middle School. She likes video games. She also likes dogs.

LEO AND ME

• ● ● ● ● ● ● ● ● ● ● ● ● ●

MYLES DALE

I've always wanted to meet my family. My mom died when I was young, and my dad left to get a slushy. I've always had a straight face. I always hung out in the alley with the cats. We all hung out in the trash can, but later that day, I heard a loud *KABOOM!* A loud crash. What was that?

All of a sudden, it got dark in our alley. All of a sudden, there was a green beam pulling me up. I was being transported somewhere. I was in a dark box. All of a sudden, I was stuck in this alien ship. But I heard a meow. It was Leo, my cat BFF. I smiled. At least I was with him. All I could hear was loud noises. "Man, this is annoying," I said to Leo. "I'm going to wander around the spacecraft thingamabob."

I was stuck in some spacecraft with my BFF, Leo the cat. I heard a thump, and these doors opened. There were aliens standing by the door. All of a sudden, they pulled out laser gun blasters that went *pew pew,* and they started shooting. But then their aim was horrible. But all of a sudden, they hit something. They hit Leo the cat. I took Leo and ran, he had a hole in him.

Part Two is coming soon/never, hehe.

MYLES DALE is a sixth grade student at Sandburg Middle School.

THE GLITCH

●●●●●●●●●●●●●●●

MIA CARLSON

Hi, Nia here, it all started one year ago when I was twelve or thirteen.

My mom and dad had been in a bad car crash when I was eleven and I had no relatives that I knew about. So I went to foster care. Then, I had to stop going to school for a while but that was fine because I was really smart. So while I was there I met some cool friends. My favorite food is like this fluffy cake. It's so good.

So a few months went by and I went back to school. And when I walked into school I had everyone looking at me and whispering about me, or teachers and students giving me special treatment. But besides that, I had really missed school and my most favorite subject was science. I loved all the cool experiments and well, everything.

One year passed, I had escaped from foster care and I had found an abandoned apartment. It had charm well, at least to me. It had been burned to the bone and they never fixed it, but it didn't get that bad. She is still in good shape. Oh, I named the apartment Bella. We have been through a lot.

Anyways, I applied for as many sports and after-school clubs as I could so I wouldn't have to go home. Name any after-school club and I was in it except for the only-boys clubs and not the math club. (I am terrible at math.)

One day it was a great day and I was on my way home

from basketball. I was exhausted and I went to bed. I woke up and I went to school but everyone was wearing all the same clothes. Was this a joke or something? And then when I got to class, my teachers did the same thing and said the same thing. I was so confused but at least I got a retry on my test. But as I was on my way home from basketball I saw something BIG!

It was like god came to me in a spaceship but instead of a god it was an alien. Jk, it was a random old lady but she looked nice. She told me that I have been given a gift. I can travel through time from the past to future. I was in shock. I stood there blank not knowing what to say or do.

I finally got the words out. I said, "WHAT!"

She said, "It's a big responsibility, are you sure you are ready?" I thought for a while and said, "Yes." That moment I knew would change my life forever.

So she took me up above the clouds and it was a beautiful sight, but it glitched and it was filled with kids my age and they were changing their minds. They were moving things with their minds, they had super speed, they were glitching here to there. So we tried for what seemed like forever but I was getting the hang of it. I learned fast so I got to go back home, but I could not tell anyone. As I walked home I realized that I could go back in time when my parents were alive to stop the car crash from happening. So the next day I went to my new future to the past.

MIA CARLSON is a sixth grade student at Sandburg Middle School.

COLOR AND EARTH

● ● ● ● ● ● ● ● ● ● ● ● ● ● ●

LAVARIA WELLS

Once upon a time, there was a girl named Quan'Niesha, but everyone called her Niesha. She was a sidekick to the most-liked superhero, but she wasn't liked too much because she was a sidekick to him. The next day out of random, the most feared villain came and demanded to see Niesha. All the students said Niesha was at home, then they gave away her address. The villain came to her door saying he kidnapped the superhero, and she needed to fight the villain in order to get him back. She agreed and went to the gym to workout. A few weeks later, it was time they fought. They started fighting and Niesha was losing. She got pushed to the ground and she was knocked out.

"Hello, is anyone there?" she called, but nobody answered. She looked up, and she wasn't on her planet. She saw things she had never seen before. She saw things like airplanes, cars, green grass, trees with leaves, and McDonald's.

She saw someone and asked, "Where am I? I have never seen green grass."

The person looked at her, confused. She said, "My name is May, and green grass is normal on Earth."

"What is Earth?" said Niesha.

May replied, "Earth is the planet we live on. What's your name? I can help you."

"I am Niesha from Planet Color. I didn't know that other planets existed," said Niesha.

May and Niesha talked, and May believed her. May searched old books for hours. She found something about the Planet Color, but the book was in a different language. Niesha said, "That's my language; I can read that."

The book said, "If someone from the Planet Color gets trapped on planet Earth, a human will have to take them back. But the human will be trapped on that planet forever and may die after two minutes."

Niesha said, "You don't have to help me."

"I will help you. If you're not from here, then you should go back," said May. Niesha didn't know how to thank her.

One week later, May and Niesha built the rocket. But before that, Niesha explored Earth. May took Niesha shopping at a mall. At the mall, they went to eat and they bought makeup, clothes, and shoes. Niesha was so happy. She had never felt this loved before. After all the fun they had, they got on the rocket. After eight hours, they got to Planet Color. Everything looked terrible. Niesha thought she was only gone for four weeks, but on Planet Color it had been four years. Niesha found the supervillain. She attacked him from behind and beat him up. He was defeated, and Niesha realized that May was still there. May was actually part of Planet Color and Earth. She was Niesha's sister. Niesha's dad had another family.

"May, I hate you. You're the reason my dad left," said Niesha.

"I'm sorry, I had no clue," said May.

They argued, then they forgave each other and lived happily on the Planet Color. They sometimes visited Earth.

LAVARIA WELLS is a sixth grader from Minneapolis. She lives in a brown house with her mom and

grandmother. On Saturdays, she loves talking on the phone with her friends. When it comes to writing, Lavaria finds grammar and taking the time to write a story hard, but she enjoys making the characters and figuring out what they're going to do.

THE DOT

● ● ● ● ● ● ● ● ● ● ● ● ● ● ● ●

BRYSON RILEA

Once there was a dot named A Dot, and that dot was playing Fortnite. Then he was hungry and he wanted some food and he eats human, so he went outside and yeah. Then he got sucked into Fortnite, so he then made a black hole and then...

He made a black hole and then he became Fortnite. But then, he got sucked into Roblox and he ate Roblox. Then, the biggest bird game out of nowhere and shot him, but he took that and became Giga Chad. Then, he ran away from Giga Chad. Then, he ran away from his mom and they played Fortnite but then...

He went to Minecraft and then he ran away from Minecraft but he was at home. And he was confused but he had people but then his house exploded because of the Roblox monster but bombs, so then he fought the Roblox master. Then, he was exploded by Two Dot and ran away but we couldn't catch him. So he went back in the portal and he lived a happy life.

BRYSON RILEA is a sixth grade student at Sandburg Middle School.

SUN GOD: THE FINAL BATTLE

• ● ● ● ● ● ● ● ● ● ● ● ● ● ● ●

DESANDRE

As a kid, The Conqueror was already showing how strong he was at the young age of 301. On his birthday, he was a happy child. Until he saw King 2.0 destroy his home planet Ziltron he decided that he would conquer THE UNIVERSE.

He traveled through the multiverse, universes, and planets, destroying everything in his path to conquer time but there was always one person in the way of The Conqueror. It was The Sun God, who has been a thorn in the side of The Conqueror since the path of destruction started. They would have crazy earth breaking battles until The Sun God Beat King 2.0 and took his energy to become THE CONQUEROR 2.0. and was fully overpowered, but Sun God had been training and becoming more and more stronger until he finally decided to confront him in his last battle of his LIFE.

The day came when The Conqueror was sitting on his throne in his kingdom, ZIltron 2.0.

Until the Sun God showed up and said, "You killed my family." He balled up his fist and said with anger in his voice, "Let's finish this."

The Conqueror slowly got up and walked towards Sun God and said, "Okay."

Sun God filled with rage and flew right into The Conqueror as the Ziltron started to shake. The Conqueror took the shot and grabbed Sun God and punched him and knocked him out. Then he took a moment to see what he had just done. He dropped down as he felt proud with a sigh of ease and confusion. He simply sat back down on his throne. As this section of the story ends we hear a menacing cry and laugh from The Conqueror.

DESANDRE lives with his brother, sister, grandma, and mom. Every Saturday he hangs out with his siblings Destiny and Deshawn and they play football together. An interesting fact is he can do the worm and he is twelve years old.

THE CURSED QUEEN

● ● ● ● ● ● ● ● ● ● ● ● ● ● ●

KEELY ADAMS

There was this city on the moon, and there was a palace with only one ruler instead of two. She was the queen, and she was immortal. She was awful to her people, but the reason why she was mean to her people was unknown. This was how it all happened: One day, this kind old lady asked the queen for a place to shelter for the night. When the queen said no, the old lady cursed her.

The queen was cursed with no voice to be spoken until she found her true love. Then, and only then, the curse would break. But she had to wait until she turned eighteen. One day, the queen took a stroll around the village and came across a man who had a wife. But the queen didn't care about his wife. The queen wanted to marry and to marry him right then and there. The only problem was she could not talk.

The queen pretended that she was a normal civilian in the village and "accidentally" bumped into him. She wrote him a note off of the tiny notepad she carried around. She wrote him a note to ask him if he wanted to go to the cafe near them, but he said no because he was married. Since he said no to the date, she wanted to chop off the wife's head. But she needed him to live. It had been two years since the curse started, and she had two more months till she would be mute forever. Until one day, a man came into the castle and asked the queen for her hand in marriage. The queen wrote on his

hand she would marry him, but she did not truly love him until she realized that he truly loved her for herself. And so she fell in love with him, and the curse was broken once and for all.

KEELY ADAMS is a sixth grade student at Sandburg Middle School.

THROUGH THE FIRE

● ● ● ● ● ● ● ● ● ● ● ● ● ● ●

Natalie Rowdon

May 6, 2178

Ring! Ring! Ring! That loud sound, like a harsh church bell, signaling the end of class woke me from my trance. I grabbed my backpack and my notebook, and performed the now so familiar walk out of the math classroom. My dreamlike state was not the cause of the subject; I quite liked math actually, but the memory of the news report I had seen only this morning. I thought back to about three hours ago as my feet automatically carried me to history. The newsanchor's voice echoed clearly across my thoughts. *"Word has just reached us of a terrible fire sweeping the land! All us humans who live here will be killed! Save yourselves!"* But no one watched the news anymore. They all were on the new apps, like NewTube, or Tick Tack. I couldn't believe some people were still worried about failing tests! I thought back to my past. Suddenly my robotic arm felt heavy. When I was very young, only three years old, I was involved in a very bad gas fire. I lost half of my body, but luckily my dad was a robotic scientist and he found me in danger. He quickly took me to his workshop and used the parts he was building for a robot to replace my body parts. I couldn't let the same thing happen to every other human. I had enough trouble surviving as a half robot in high school. I knew not everyone's parents could do the

same things my dad could. I could lose everyone. I had to do something.

May 10, 2178

I had spent the last four days thinking of what I could do to help. I am not a brave person, I'm more of the type who is super smart and gets good grades and is known for it. The brain, not the brawn. And it has nothing to do with my robot parts. My brain is completely human. But enough about that. I had no idea what to do! I mean, I was still trying to find my way in *high school*. How could I save millions of people from a giant fire! Before this, my biggest problems were school bullies and being myself! And worse still, everyone I try to warn thinks I'm crazy! "It's 2178!" they say. "We've been around for centuries. No big fire will happen now!" And my robot sides give them even more proof. You've seen the movies! All robots ever do is take over. They don't take me seriously because they think I'm crazy! And my robot eye is even more nerve racking. Yes, I have a robot eye. A red special sensor that lets me see who they really are. A piece of technology that my dad is especially proud of. I just look at anyone, and I can see who they are inside, nice or mean. It's like a pie graph. I look, and their soul says like, 30 percent bad, 70 percent good. So I know that they're a good person!

May 18, 2178

I know what happened! Turns out, there are some evil robots in the world! They started the fire, and they actually deleted the news report! So I told my close friends, and they believed me, so we put our heads together and came up with two plans. My three friends Eleanor, Feven, and Ryan have found the lair of the robots that started the fire. They are going to defeat them, because they have cool disabilities like me. Feven has ADHD, and so she can be immensely focused and she is great at fighting techniques. Eleanor lost her hand,

and so my father made her a special mechanical hand that moves ten times faster than normal and is like a wolverine claw! And Ryan looks so sweet, but she's a feisty little fire! She'll bring your guard crashing down with her cute little antics, and then strike hard and bring *you* crashing down! And me and Nailah, who is also half robot, made these giant water sprayers with parts from my dad's lab and we found twenty other robots to help us spray them across the continent! We will conquer this! The fire happens later today. Now or never!

May 19, 2178

Yes! We did it! The continent is saved and I won't lose the people I love! Life is great. And now, I think I truly know myself. I am the brave half robot who helped save the world! And no one can say anything to change that. Not even the meanest bully. And that's my story.

NATALIE ROWDON is a sixth grade student at Sandburg Middle School. She loves to dance, play soccer, and do gymnastics. She also loves to flip and kick and cartwheel all around! Natalie wants a good education, so she wants to go to University of Minnesota or an Ivy League school. And though most people say that as you get older you get less flexible, Natalie is eleven and this is the first year she has been able to do a backbend!

JUST NORMAL
BRANDON

How did it happen? I don't know. When did it happen? Yesterday. Okay, let me back you up a day. So I'm Brandon, just a normal kid in a normal world. . . or so I thought. So yesterday I was in school and the bell rang and school was over. I went outside and was going to walk home, but to get home you have to go through the forest. So I went in and I was just walking when I heard a tree branch break. *CRACK!* I spun around but there was nothing. I kept walking but more cautiously. Then out of nowhere *BANG!* And after that I remember nothing. I woke up about an hour later and walked home the rest of the night was normal. When I woke up the next morning I discovered *I had powers.*

So I had the power to read people's minds. I figured that out because I went downstairs and a speech bubble was above my moms head but she couldn't see it. I could see what she was thinking! I thought I was going crazy or hallucinating. But when I got to school everyone had one above their head but they couldn't see it. Then I remembered what happened yesterday after school. I thought that could have been what caused it. After school I went to investigate the forest for clues. I found this weird goo substance. I didn't know what it was so I brought it home. I was at home investigating and it

seemed like it wanted to go somewhere. So I went to where it wanted to go, but then it stopped and tried to go up. I looked up and there was an alien UFO. I ran and didn't look back. I got home and went to bed. Next morning I had a few tests at school. I could see all the intelligent people and see their answers. I did so well on all of the tests. I loved these powers. But then I saw some thoughts that I didn't like. They were talking about me and how stupid I was. So I left. Then I went to find the aliens. After hours of searching I found them. I asked them to take my powers away. They said yes then they said they never meant to give them to me in the first place so they took them away and I was normal again how I liked it. Just normal Brandon.

FINN J. is a sixth grade student at Sandburg Middle School. He loves to play sports and board games. Finn also loves fruit. He has no idea why but he just loves it. Any kind is delicious.

THE ADVENTURES OF SOUL AND QUEEN

MARIAH YOUNGMARK

One day on the planet Uranus there was a girl who was named S0ul. She was sitting on her couch with her sidekick Queen. They were evil because they hate Chadomoth, Chadomoth is the good guy but they hate him because he always gets in their way. They were bored and decided to grab a bunch of monkeys from a zoo and hang them over lava which was already in their secret lair. They then hacked all television programs and showed all the monkeys in the background because it looked funny to them.

After they hacked it they said, "Chadomoth has six hours to come to the secret lair or else they would destroy a building." Somehow Chadomoth got there in one minute.

Chadomoth said, "Let those monkeys go."

S0ul and Queen laughed at him and said "No." But little did they know Chadomoth had super speed and he grabbed the monkeys and freed them. S0ul and Queen started crying because they wanted to drown them in the lava. Chadomoth started laughing at them. They got so angry they started seeing red and turning red.

S0ul and Queen started pounding and breaking everything they could. Chadomoth said, "Sorry not sorry." S0ul and Queen got so sick of him and attacked him.

And Chadomoth was crying so bad. But they didn't care. After they finished with him, they destroyed the tower. But they made sure hours before there was no one in the tower because they don't like hurting people, just Chadomoth.

MARIAH YOUNGMARK has five brothers and two sisters. Another thing about Mariah is that for a career she would love to be a fashion designer so she can make clothes that she's happy with, and so whenever she needs a certain piece of clothing she could make it. Also, Mariah loves fashion and exploring new ways to style herself. One more thing about Mariah is that on a Saturday she likes to lay in her bed watching TikTok all alone in her room. It's nice and peaceful.

THE MIDNIGHT MONSTER

• • • • • • • • • • • • • • •

ZEB MIGUEL

It was night at 3 a.m., and Jacob was walking. A wight monster came out one of the graves and said, "Bum bum bum da da da," and Jacob ran. The monster grew humongous.

Jacob saw someone and said, "Help!"

The boy said, "Huh, what?"

Jacob said, "Look!"

The boy saw the monster and said, "What is that?"

Jacob said, "I don't know, but he is coming fast and we have to run fast."

Jacob and the boy ran as fast as they could. The whole city of New York saw the humongous monster. The NYPD got the suited men with SWAT gear and a truck with a laser on it and tried to shoot the monster but the monster punched all the big screens in Time Square. It started an electric fire at a nearby building and the SWAT called a tank and left it running for later in an alleyway.

Jacob and the boy got in the tank and blinded the monster with the laser. Jacob and the boy and the NYPD tied up the monster and send him into space and never saw him again.

ZEB MIGUEL is a sixth grade student at Sandburg Middle School.

WILLOW, BRUNO, AND MLK

● ● ● ● ● ● ● ● ● ● ● ● ● ● ●

"Another day, another slay," said Willow. Yes it was. "But we should get some rest," said Bruno. And then they both went to sleep.

The next morning, Bruno and Willow woke up and ate breakfast. But all of a sudden *BEEP BEEP BEEP,* their watches were going off.

"You know what that means!" said Bruno. They both ran to the computer and saw that there was a mission. Willow and Bruno have this occupation where they time travel to save the future. This mission was to save Martin Luther King, Jr. He did not feel like he should do the speech.

Willow and Bruno grabbed all that they would need. Willow and Bruno set their watches to the right time and hit the button. *POW!* They were time traveling. They went back to just before Martin Luther King, Jr., was going to do his speech. When they got there he looked very worried. Willow asked what's wrong. He looked at her in confusion and asked, "Who are you?"

"Hi! I am Willow and this is Bruno. We are here to help you," said Willow."

"Help me? What do you mean 'help me?'" MLK asked.

"We know that you are second-guessing yourself on doing your speech," said Bruno firmly.

"Yes I know, but I just dont think it's good enough. I mean, I don't think it will change anything–" "Let me see the speech," Willow interrupted.

She thought the speech was great. After a while of talking to MLK, Willow and Bruno convinced him to do the speech. When they were done preparing, he went out there and did GREAT! The speech was awesome sauce. Willow and Bruno's work was done. They clicked the button so that they could go back home. Once they arrived home they celebrated. They had pizza and cake. Willow's cheeks were hurting, smiling from one side of her face to the other.

OLIVIA U. is a sixth grade student at Sandburg Middle School. Some things about her are that she has a dog named Kaiko. This is how you say her name *KAY-co*, but Olivia calls her Potato. Kaiko is all black, and her chest is white, and her paws are brindle brown. When Olivia grows up, she would love to be an entrepreneur, or something big like a doctor, a cosmetologist, or gymnast. She likes doing gymnastics and is on a team. She also likes softball.

THE FUTURE NOW AND BACK THEN

MIZAYE WOODS

B ack in the future, there were technology basketball courts everywhere. I went to them often. It was so easy and fun and simple, so other people started coming more and more until it was night time. We were playing lots of games only because we were using my ball.

So then I went inside a basketball court and I started to play really good. People started noticing me playing basketball and so many people wanted to play for their team. So I did. There was one team that I knew had a whole lot of technological stuff on the basketball courts. Then I got to play a game. I had dropped at least seventy to 100 points a game. It was so easy. Then an NBA player came. He was so good he was the GOAT, so I had to show off. Then he gave me a card.

For his NBA team I went to the spot of the team, and then he gave me a technology suit to wear on the court for the games. I will tell you that I became the best basketball player in the whole world. For real! Then I went back in time where they did not have the same things. Anyways, it was too hard to play this game. It was like I was going against myself back there. I couldn't do this. I had become a noob. I wanted to go back.

MIZAYE WOODS is a sixth grade student at Sandburg Middle School. His favorite food is chicken wings, because they are delicious! His favorite sports are basketball and football. His favorite way to spend a Saturday is to play in a basketball tournament, watch other friends play some games, and then go home to relax.

QUINTESSA

●━●━●━●━●━●━●━●━●━●━●━●━●

LILLY SOUVANNARATH

Hi, my name is Rosie, and my plan is to take over my
home planet. Well, the only reason I'm doing this is
to get back at my family. Like, I love my family, but
they never notice me. So that is why I'm gonna take over my
home planet. Anyway, the first step to my evil plan is to find
something to help me take over the planet. When I was doing my research, I found out that there is a powerful crystal
on Mars. Wait, my super villain name is Quintessa. But back
to the plan. The second step is to use my parent's spaceship
and go to Mars. Step three: Once I get to Mars, I'm going
to steal the crystal, but there's one small problem. There are
always people watching out for the crystal just in case people
take it, just like I'm trying to do. But of course, I always have
a plan. All I gotta do is sneak in and be careful. That's my plan
when I get to Mars. I'm leaving for Mars tomorrow.

When I got on the ship, I literally didn't understand anything. *Okay Rosie, you got this!* That's what I keep saying to
myself. After like twenty minutes, I got the ship to work.
Okay Rosie, you can do this! After all the traveling, I finally made it to Mars. Okay, all I need to do is get that crystal
now! As I'm sneaking into the palace, I see a lot of guards
guarding the crystal. I'm feeling a bit uptight, like it feels like
a bunch of little ants are crawling around, protecting their
food. And if I do anything, they would try to get all over

me. But I can't let my feelings distract me right now. *Let's see, what should I do? How can I get that crystal?*

I'm thinking about all this stuff I can do, but it would probably get me caught. As I'm looking around for something I could use as a distraction, I hear a lot of guards saying to each other that they are really hungry. So I sneak behind some of the guards and go to a door that no guards are near. I yell in a deep voice, "ATTENTION ALL GUARDS! THERE IS A FEAST DOWNSTAIRS FOR ALL OF YOU!"

Then, after all of that, all the guards go rushing and pushing each other to go downstairs. *Okay Rosie, this should give you at least ten minutes to get that gem and leave.* So I go as quickly as I can to get that crystal and leave. But as I'm walking back to my spaceship, one of the guards sees me. I get into my ship as fast as lighting. The guard starts to call for backup. As my ship starts to finally work, they all start shooting at me! Right when I think I was rid of them, I see another spaceship shooting at me!

I got rid of them after all the trouble. When I got back to my secret evil lair, I had to see how I would use this crystal to take over the world. I was doing my research when I found out that all I have to do is wait until sunrise and hold it to the sky on the center of the planet. Then the crystal will make me the most powerful being in the entire universe. So all day, I was getting ready for sunrise and getting all my stuff to take over the world. Now I just needed to get in my spaceship and go to the center of my home planet. I finally made it to the center and only a few more minutes until sunrise. When I was about to hold up the crystal some stupid superhero came out of nowhere.

"Hey stop there!" the superhero said.

"Who are you?" I said.

"My name is Hope because I'm always there to help!"

"Whatever, just leave me alone!" I replied. Right when I was about to hold the crystal, the superhero took it right out of my hands.

"Hey, give that back to me!" I shouted.

"No you can't do this, if you do this what would it do for you?!"

"To be honest I really don't care about taking over the planet. All I wanted was to make my parents mad," I said.

She was just wasting my time, so I took out my laser gun and started shooting at her. But she was too fast for me.

"Hey stop, I'm not here to fight you." Hope said.

"Then why are you here?" I said, as I kept shooting at her. Sunrise was almost about to end. *I have to hurry,* I thought in my head.

"I'm here to tell you that there are better ways to figure out your problems," Hope said in a calming voice. As she came closer to me I was about to start shooting again but when I was about to she gave me a hug. Something felt weird in my stomach like everything felt nice inside.

"I never had a hug in my life." I said then I started noticing tears coming down from my face. " Hey, it's okay I'm here, you can tell me anything if you want," Hope said as me and her sat down. Sunrise was over and there was nothing for me to do now. And out of nowhere I just started to break down. I felt like everything I did was stupid.

After talking with Hope, I felt a lot better. So after everything I gave back the crystal and I decided to give my parents a visit. *Okay Rosie, you can do this.* I was saying to myself as I was knocking on the door. When the door opened I saw an old woman and when she looked at me she started crying.

"Mom, is that you?" I said with tears falling down.

"Yes, yes it is, honey. I missed you so much," she said. After finally making up with my family and them apologizing to me, I felt good about myself and happy to have my family back.

LILLY SOUVANNARATH is a sixth grade student at Sandburg Middle School. Her favorite food is pizza. Her favorite sport to play and watch is basketball. What she likes about writing is that she gets to make her own story the way she wants it to be.

THE SPACESHIP

• • ● • ● ● • ● ● ● • ● ● ● • ● ●

MARCUS STAMPP

M e and Opti Jr. flew to the planet Kepler 626b and immediately a giant boulder came whooshing down from the air and separated me and Opti Jr. Since the planet had zero gravity, we went flying to the other side of the planet. I was really nervous at first because I've never actually been anywhere without Opti Jr. He was my translator.

So I just started walking and after running 3 miles in one minute (yes, I am really fast) I saw a broken up spaceship. Opti Jr. didn't know that I actually knew how to fix spaceships (how convenient).

0.2 seconds later, I finished fixing the spaceship and went inside. There was a big red button that said: LAUNCH (and then in very fine print) Emergency only press this button if you know how to drive a spaceship!

And then right after I pressed the button, I started going up really fast and realized that I didn't know how to drive. I started looking for an instruction manual and I read the AREA that had 51 steps on how to use a spaceship. Seven microseconds later I knew all about how to use a spaceship, but I forgot about Opti Jr. (I forget about a lot of stuff, okay!).

It was perfect timing because right when I looked down I saw Opti Jr. and he also saw me. He flew up as fast as he

could and stopped the spaceship, and then we flew back to our planet: Kepler 111b.

MARCUS STAMPP is a sixth grade student at Sandburg Middle School.

OPTI JR. GETS REVENGE

● ● ● ● ● ● ● ● ● ● ● ● ● ●

AHMED M.

Once upon a time on a planet called Kepler 111B, the main character was named Opti Jr. His father died, so he was going to get the good guy who attacked him. The guy's name was Mazen. He used a ray gun on Opti's dad, so now Opti is out to get revenge.

He makes a device to track down the person who killed his father. He makes a giant wand that would change anything into an ant. Then, they located where Mazen lived. They found him and then they are going to use the wand. They used the wand but it said it would take six days. He lived on Earth but there were humans who lived there.

"They can't change the humans or my planet might get destroyed. My mom would die, my best friends would die," Opti said. So they decided to tell the government to clear Asia out so they didn't die. And that's how I got revenge and saved the Earth from turning into ants.

AHMED M. is a sixth grade student at Sandburg Middle School. Ahmed likes sports. His favorite food

165

is rice with chicken, and bananas. He also likes to play video games with his friends.

THE CURSE AND THE CURE

●●●●●●●●●●●●●●●

SHAYDEN COLE THURMAN

Diary I: How I came to be

I was starving almost to death. The witch cursed me. She worked with my father to curse me. I was always hungry for food no matter how much food I consumed. I needed to break the curse. I wanted to find my father and show my father how it feels to be hungry for flesh at every single second of his pathetic life. I wanted to watch him suffer and find out how it feels!

Diary II: Finding something that can help me find my father

The witch may be helpful in finding my father. I will find that wicked fiend.

I asked the locals in the area to see what they had to say. They said at midnight on the dot the witch will come to you if you perform a satanic ritual you can summon her. I wanted to perform it because she could help me locate my father.

I lit the candles. The witch arrived.

The witch said, "Hello my child, what do you need me for?"

"I need you to help me find my father and help me break the cures you put on me," I said.

"I have a good reason for that if people summon me and I must do what they say," she said. "Where is my father?" I asked.

"He is hiding in the mountains somewhere deep in the snow cave. Go there and you shall find him, my child," she told me.

Diary III: I found him.

The witch said, "With that said and done, I will break the curse. It was a jolly good time working with you."

I am in the mountains, going toward the snow caves. But first I will ask the locals for their ships because this would be a long journey. I might as well use the ship of the locals. They just said yes and let me have it. I started up the ship, and wow, this thing went fast. Good thing I had an instructor to guide me. Okay, I found the snow cave. I put dynamite on the walls just in case things got ugly. I found my father. He was in hiding.

"You coward! Come out and face me," I said.

"Fine, you win," he replied.

We both ran at each other fists ready. Sadly I didn't see the fact that he had more muscle than me, so I backed up and ran out of the snow cave. My father thought he won but with a push of a button an avalanche started in the cave. Well, I had my revenge. That felt sweet, *finally!*

SHAYDEN COLE THURMAN is a sixth grade student at Sandburg Middle School.

TINA AND THE DRAGONS

● ● ● ● ● ● ● ● ● ● ● ● ● ●

ADELYN VU

O nce upon a time, there was a human girl named Tina, and her nickname was Tin. Her hobbies she liked were singing and dancing. She really wanted to find her parents. That was her only wish. Her parents disappeared when she was only ten. Now she was on a mission to find them.

She was trying to escape the orphanage. This orphanage she was at was really rude, because she was the only normal one there. The "people" in the orphanage weren't normal except for her. Because they were all dragons! But she only had two people that really cared about her that used to be there with her. Her missing parents did. Tina missed when they tucked her in at night. She couldn't sleep if she kept thinking about them. Where did they go? Did they leave her on purpose? This orphanage was really dark. Ever since Tina arrived everything shut down. There was silence. But she couldn't get along with the others because they were dragons! She was wondering if she could try to fit in with the dragons. Would they change if she tried to fit in? Tina asked the dragons to be her friend.

"Hi, would you like to be my friend?"

ADELYN VU is a sixth grade student at Sandburg Middle School. She lives in Golden Valley, Minn.

MAKING IT INTO GAMES

● ● ● ● ● ● ● ● ● ● ● ● ● ● ● ● ●

CHRISTOPHER CLARK

Once upon a time there was a kid named Asher. His house was blue. He had a happy life and his parents were held for ransom. He couldn't pay it, so the guy on the phone sounded intimidating and killed them. Asher started feeling sad and when he woke up one morning he felt like his blood cells were burning. He couldn't get up for a while, but he had to. As he went up the ages, he got used to the feeling. He is twenty-four now. He's got the power. The power is that he starts shooting fire attacks and they penetrate the wall. *CRASH!* He usually doesn't let people know about his powers. He finds a card on the floor and it says "join this game and you could win fame and money." He does it and a jet flies to him to pick him up. And now he is flying to an island called World's Edge. Now he is at the island and they're explaining the game and it's all for the theme "selfless." You have one teammate and they could be a teammate that helps you or leaves you, so you always want a teammate that you know and trust.

CHRISTOPHER CLARK aka Chris, is a sixth grade student at Sandburg Middle School. He lives with his brother and his dad in a small house. His favorite sport

is American football. He also loves ribs because they are tasty.

THE CRY OF BLOB CITY

● ● ● ● ● ● ● ● ● ● ● ● ● ● ●

KENNEDI FRANCOIS

One day three neighborhood friends were walking home together.

"I hope my mom will let us have a sleepover," Jet said.

"That would be awesome, my little brother is so annoying I need a day out of the house," Oliver said. The three friends made their way home but soon noticed a new path off the regular way to their houses.

"Hey hold up, let's take this path, " said Emma. The path was colored bright green so it was hard to miss. As Emma led the others down the path they noticed some kind of moving slime blob.

"Hey do you see that?" Oliver said.

"Yeah, let's go check it out," stated Jet.

The three friends raced down the path and moved their way toward the blob.

"Hey, I'm Mr. Twiddle and I need your help!"

"What the Fortnite?"

"Blob City is in trouble and I'm melting by the second. I'm the only one left of my kind and I can't die, not now."

"Blob City, where's that?"

"Well it's hard to explain, but for now follow me."

Mr. Twiddle told them that they had to teleport to 2584 where Blob City is located. They were walking deep in the forest and soon made it.

"Woah, it's glowing," said Jet.

"What is that?" Emma said.

"It's our way to the year 2584," Twiddle said. They jumped in the glowing purple portal and soon made it in the middle of the city.

"You ain't kidding when you said Blob City is in danger," said Oliver. All the buildings were slowly collapsing and there was so much debris in the sky. "Woah look at the flying cars, this is insane."

The city was futuristic and full of new things to Emma, Oliver, and Jet.

"We don't have much time, let's get to work," said Twiddle.

They raced to catch up to Twiddle.

"So what exactly is the plan?" said Jet.

"Well," said Twiddle, rolling out a map, "we're here," he pointed to the middle of the map where there were drawings of buildings. "We need to get here," and he pointed to a tiny place in the corner.

"The thing is," Twiddle started to speak. "The reason buildings are falling is because of the dragon's cry. He is in pain and the only way to make him stop is to get a special liquid from his eye and if i drink it. I will stop melting."

"Well what are we waiting for?" Emma blurted. They hiked their way up the mountain until they found themselves waiting outside a cave.

"Well kids, we made it."

The dragon's cry was loud and ugly. It was a deep unholy moan that filled the city.

"This seems dangerous."

"I don't feel too well."

"Stop being a baby," Emma said.

As they headed in the cave the cry grew louder and soon the ground started to shake. Twiddle splashed some kind of liquid on the dragon and it began to calm down and fall asleep. "Hurry, we don't have much time until it wears out," said Twiddle.

"What do you need us to do?"

"Okay, here's the plan. Emma and Jet take this rope. Oliver and I are going to extract the liquid while you hold us up there by having the rope around our waist."

"Got it!" said Oliver.

After they got the liquid they put it in a necklace and the dragon started to wake.

"Hurry, get us down," yelled Twiddle. Emma and Jet used all their might and soon got them off. They rushed out of the cave and once they were out Twiddle started to drink the liquid.

"I'm not surrounded by a big puddle anymore, it worked," Twiddle said.

"Yay!" the kids exclaimed. They hiked back down the mountain and saw the buildings were not falling anymore.

"Thank you so much for helping me save Blob City," Twiddle said.

"No problem," the kids replied.

The four said their goodbyes and Twiddle opened a portal for them to go back. And the rest of Blob City and Twiddle lived happily ever after. And for the three kids they made it back safely and ended up having the sleepover.

KENNEDI FRANCOIS is a sixth grade student that attends Sandburg Middle School. She has two dogs and a cat and loves them very much. In school Kennedi is very smart, outside of school she is always busy with sports but when she is not on the court she is watching *Dance Moms* and spending time with friends and family.

EDUCATOR RESOURCES

●●●●●●●●●●●●●●●●●●

THE SLOW BURN OF SUSPENSE

● ● ● ● ● ● ● ● ● ● ● ● ● ● ● ●

By Cristeta Boarini and Ellen Fee

Number of sessions: Four

End product: Detailed, three-paragraph (minimum) short story in the mystery and suspense genre
Literary devices and English Language Arts skills explored:

- Plot development
- Sensory and descriptive language
- Revision and editing

Young people want to write scary stories. Think back to your own childhood and some of these moments might sound familiar: an older sibling trying to spook you with a ghost story before bedtime, teenagers whispering urban legends around a bonfire, a friend telling a creepy tale with a flashlight lit under her chin at a sleepover.

On one hand, suspenseful stories can simply be fun—your heart races, you gasp, you breathe a sigh of relief when the hero escapes the evil creature's clutches. But on a deeper level, these kinds of stories can also empower us to confront

our fears—imaginary ones, like a monster under the bed, or very real ones, like a school bully—in a safe and healthy way, where the authors (your students) are in control of their narrative from beginning to end.

One challenge that often emerges with student writers, especially in this type of project, is the tendency to launch right into the action and speed through the plot and resolution, leaving elements like character development, rising action, and narrative tone underdeveloped.

This lesson plan encourages student writers to approach their stories more holistically—creating a setting that evokes a mysterious tone, brainstorming details about how the main character is feeling, and building suspense through pacing and word choice.

Student writers will enjoy the chance to lean in to their spooky sides, craft a plot and resolution that satisfies their curiosities, and share their stories with their peers.

SESSION ONE: INTRODUCTION TO MYSTERY AND SUSPENSE GENRE

We always start a unit of writing by diving into some model texts. What we found most helpful was to present students with both a professional model text and a student-written model text. The first example is meant to exemplify the genre, and the second helps students grasp how they might translate the genre into their own writing and skill level.

For the professional example in mystery and suspense, we listened to "Multo" by Samuel Marzioli, as read by Levar Burton on the actor's titular podcast. The text can also be found online in Apex Magazine's archives. The story follows a Filipino American man as he recalls a childhood encounter

with an evil spirit. For the student example, we read "Willa and the Mysterious Forest Trail," a short story written by eighth grader Mumtaz and published in 826 MSP's Fall 2022 chapbook *The Tree That We All Grow On*.

We specifically chose stories that did not need to rely on action or gore to advance the story. "Multo" especially luxuriates in the build-up, using sensory language to turn even the most mundane family garage or childhood bedroom into chambers of terror. In addition, "Multo" and student model texts are written in more contemporary, accessible language with more diverse perspectives compared to a classic mystery story written by Edgar Allen Poe or Sir Arthur Conan Doyle.

In this anthology, "The Search" by Dre Johnston and "Where's Rachel?" by Sophia Xiong would serve as excellent student model texts.

SESSION TWO: BRAINSTORMING

A key part of building up suspense lies in sensory details: what a character sees, hears, smells, touches, or tastes as they experience the story. To help students brainstorm, we used a graphic organizer to help students examine even the most trivial minutiae of their stories' setting. We asked them not only where the story takes place, but when, what things are making noise, what details can be seen, what the character feels both physically and emotionally.

We wanted to push the students to ramp up their vocabulary for this project. Before they got down to brainstorming individually, had them build a spooky word bank together as a group. On the whiteboard in the classroom, we made four columns titled with the following categories: setting, noun, adjective, verb. Every student was given a few sticky notes and was asked to post their ideas for each category. As a

group, we were able to imagine the abandoned hospitals, desolate barns, and creepy coffee shops that you can read about in this book. Students took a bit of fiendish pleasure in coming up with the most unique ideas—especially if they could gross out the rest of the class.

Session Three: Writing

With spooky details ready to go, students were raring to write. But a key lesson we wanted students to takeaway is that great suspense writing takes its time. It's not nonstop action all the time, explosions and jump scares galore. Suspenseful writing makes use of the dim moonlight, the creak of a stair, the touch of a breeze.

One classic way to encourage students to inject detail and description into their writing is the concept of "show, don't tell." For this project, we defined "show, don't tell" as using description of the setting, action, or character's traits to illustrate what's going on rather than saying it plainly or directly. Here's a pair of examples:

TELL: I walked through the woods. It was already fall, and I felt cold.

SHOW: The dry, orange leaves crunched under my feet as I pulled the collar up on my coat.

In class, students discussed how "dry, orange leaves" signal to the reader that we're in autumn, while pulling the collar up on one's coat signifies that the character is reacting to something chilly. We took the example one step further by doing a quick compare-and-contrast exercise with professional and student-written work. We took a handful of spooky and suspenseful "show, don't tell" example paragraphs from writers like Stephen King and Tomi Adeyemi, as well as example

paragraphs of silly superhero stories written by second grade students. The paragraphs were printed out on individual notecards, and in small groups students organized the examples into "show" versus "tell" categories.

With all this background information, students were instructed to write their suspense story in a minimum of three paragraphs, and to specifically include some "show, don't tell" descriptions. Out of all the genres we explored with students during the 2022-23 school year, this suspense story was the one they were most excited to try. Multiple times we heard students share that they had never had the opportunity to write a story like this before. Students who struggled to even write a stanza in a previous poetry unit were churning out paragraphs when they could be free to include all the detail they wanted, and when the story could go wherever it took them.

SESSION FOUR: REVISION

Even when the writing is at its most inspiring and enjoyable, revision is often the part of the process to which many young people are the most averse. Reactions range from "my story is perfect as-is," to "I already did the work, why do I need to redo it?"

Writing can always be improved. One example we love to show students is Kate DiCamillo's first draft of her award-winning novel, *Because of Winn-Dixie*. Scholastic has an easy-to-search PDF of what the first page of her first draft looks like. In the draft, nothing is capitalized properly, there are no paragraph breaks anywhere. And when comparing the draft's first page to the published version's first page, the content is wildly different and improved in the copy that made it to press.

This example helps to show young people that great writing—even from professional authors—doesn't arrive on the page perfect and fully formed, like Athena bursting from Zeus' head. Perfection takes multiple tries, and is worth it in the end.

With that practical explanation of revision, we then made the revision process even more worthwhile by putting every young person's biggest motivation on the line: winning candy. Revision suddenly became so much more doable when Twix and Twizzlers were involved. So instead of handing the students a rubric with required revisions, we gave them bingo cards.

Revision Bingo takes the popular game of chance and attaches various revision suggestions to the numbers, so that in order to win a student must not only have a BINGO, but must also complete a series of edits. All the edits and their associated bingo numbers are listed on a reference sheet that the students have with them as they play. For example, if the number B-1 is called, students who have that number on their cards must also complete the corresponding edit "Find one place to add a new adjective to your writing."

Other examples include:

B-1 Find one place to add a new adjective to your writing.
B-2 Double check for capital letters at the beginnings of your sentences.
B-3 Double check for capital letters on names and other proper nouns.
B-4 Find one word that you can replace with a show-don't-tell example.
B-5 Find a place to add an onomatopoeia (sound effect).
I-16 Add a transition word or phrase to the beginning of a sentence.

I-17 Double check for missing punctuation at the ends of your sentences.
I-18 Rewrite your beginning sentence to really grab the reader's attention.
I-19 Find a place where you are missing a comma in one of your sentences.

. . . and so on.

There are many free bingo card generators online to create a bingo card that fits your needs. In our version, we customized the traditional "Free Space" to say "Write a Title."

This was a huge success, fueled by M&M's and Skittles as the bingo counters with larger candy prizes for the winners. Instead of revision being a dreaded exercise, gamifying it not only made the process fun, but also bore fruitful results in the students' stories.

. . .

If you are interested in more engaging writing lessons—including the prompt "Time Travel Is Nerve Wracking," which inspired the science fiction stories in this book—head over to 826digital.com for myriad prompts and projects written by educators and implemented with real students. Every lesson plan includes model texts from young people.

ABOUT THE SCHOOL

The sixth graders in this book all attend Sandburg Middle School, a sixth-eighth grade learning center located in Golden Valley, Minn., a Twin Cities inner-ring suburb.

Originally opened in 1959 and named for Swedish American author Carl Sandburg, the middle school closed in 2010 and reopened in 2018. About 600 students attend the school each year.

Sandburg Middle School is dedicated to providing a rigorous, supportive education that prepares all students for Advanced Placement courses in high school and teaches them the skills needed to positively contribute to their community.

As a full service community school, Sandburg promotes academic excellence by offering an array of health and social services to students, families and community. The school is a community hub that helps meet the diverse needs of students, their families and the neighborhood. The partner offerings in full service community schools are open to everyone.

ABOUT 826 MSP

826 MSP is a nonprofit youth writing center that amplifies the voices, stories, and power of K–12, Black, Indigenous, and students of color through writing, publishing, and leadership programs. The organization was founded in 2009 in response to Minnesota's opportunity gap, and continues to work toward ending inequities in education. Our youth writing center, located in South Minneapolis, provides a safe, welcoming creative space with a whimsical "oceanographic" theme. We sincerely believe that a fun, beautiful space helps to inspire, hone, and broadcast students' creativity.

In 2019, 826 MSP became the ninth chapter of 826 National, a network of youth writing and tutoring centers in major cities throughout the United States. 826 National's philosophy is that individualized attention is critical to improving literacy and equipping students for success. We work toward our mission and serve our community through the following programs:

After-School Writing Lab: This program serves about fourty students per semester. Hosted four days a week, we pair volunteer tutors one-on-one with students to offer academic support across all subjects. Each session also offers students thirty minutes of dedicated writing practice to help cultivate students' skills.

Field Trips: Available to first-fifth grade public school classes, our field trips strive to embolden our next generation of writers to explore and value their own voice. Students and teachers join us for one of two field trip experiences: Storytelling & Bookmaking or Poetry Navigators. Volunteers work with the student authors to create a book during the field trip.

Summer Writing Workshops: Held in July and August for a variety of ages and interests, each workshop represents a collaboration between student authors, volunteers, and community partners working to create original pieces around a theme, while also incorporating key writing and communication skills to prevent the "summer slide."

Writers' Room: 826 MSP works in concert with staff and students at South High School to create a drop-in writing center within the school for all their writing needs. For teachers, this includes lesson plan support and project ideas, and for students this includes help with college essay writing, homework assignments, and personal writing projects.

Young Authors' Book Project: Classroom teachers, volunteers, and 826 MSP staff work together to support students in the creative process of writing original works around a theme. Illustrators, designers, publishers, and printers, collaborate with students to create a professionally published anthology of their work.

Young Authors' Council: 826 MSP's youth leadership program connects teens through writing and civic engagement. Each school year, the program offers up to fifteen youth a paid fellowship, publishing opportunities, and leadership experience. YAC is open to students in grades 7-12 who attend Twin Cities metro schools.

ACKNOWLEDGEMENTS

ACKNOWLEDGEMENTS

• • • • • • • • • • • • • • •

Whether you are currently a sixth grader, or you've paged through this book with middle school memories swirling through your mind, you know that sixth grade especially is a momentous time. Bodies are growing, friendships changing, and the taste of independence is starting to become particularly sweet. Not to mention there's still everything going on at home, more classwork than ever, and suddenly you have to get from your locker to class all within four minutes?!

In the midst of all that, the sixth graders of Sandburg Middle School arrived at the challenge of putting together a whole book with what can only be pure magic. Classes spent writing with them brought unprecedented joy, boundless creativity, and a whole lot of goofiness. But the most awe-inspiring thing these eleven- and twelve-year-olds did for four months was to share. Share their ideas, their favorite TV shows, their candy, their hairstyling tips. . . and ultimately share themselves fully to make this book and these stories possible. As you hold this book now, please understand the gift that it is. These brilliant young authors have trusted us with their words, and we honor them for making this book beautiful, bountiful, and undoubtedly theirs.

In the spirit of thanks, we would like to express our gratitude. . .

To Shelby Dale DeWeese—wearing both hats of sixth grade English teacher and 826 MSP board member in this project—who led our crew with high expectations and high enthusiasm throughout. Your constant kindness and steady hand, even on days that were not always fun, ensured that every student was able to participate as best they could. We are so grateful that you are part of the 826 community.

To all our volunteers who help 826 MSP deliver our free programs, but especially to Marlin A. Jenkins, Frances Strahan, Ava Warford, Zoe Jagiela, Erin McDonagh, Stacy Carroll Swearingen, and Ashley Lustig for working with students in person. Your impact could be seen every session when students would cheer, greet you by name, or even just quietly read you their story with pride. Without you, this book would not have been nearly as fun, nor as meaningful. Additional thanks to Elizabeth Daugherty, Marley Richmond, Elyssia Nguyen, and Valarie Paul for their proofreading prowess and helping our students' authentic voices get on the page.

To 826 MSP's staff, including Jamal Adam, Cristeta Boarini, Ellen Fee, Annie Chen, and Aminah Hussein, who understand deeply that caring adults, creative curriculum, and student-centered vision make for a wonderful community of writers.

To Wise Ink Creative Publishing, especially Dara Beevas and Nyle Vialet. It's so rare to find creative partners who truly *get it* when it comes to our unique blend of whimsy and community building. Working with you all is a joy we look forward to every year.

To 826 MSP's committed and visionary board of directors, and the community that continues to support us, especially Breck School, 826 National, the Cuttlefish Society, Otto Bremer Trust, the ECMC Foundation, and the Walser

Foundation. Your support ensures our students' fantastical stories can make their way into the world.

This activity is made possible by the voters of Minnesota through a Minnesota State Arts Board Operating Support grant, thanks to a legislative appropriation from the Arts and Cultural Heritage Fund.

LAND ACKNOWLEDGEMENT

Today, 11 tribal nations and communities are located within the state of Minnesota—the place 826 MSP calls home. 826 MSP pays tribute to the Dakota and Ojibwe as the original people of this sacred land, first called Mni Sota Makoce in the Dakota language.

Mni Sota Makoce is a place that carries a deep, layered history across the thousands of years the Dakota and Ojibwe peoples have been in kinship with the land, and in the centuries since European settlers colonized the land that the state of Minnesota now occupies. The land seizures and genocide committed by the United States were projects of spiritual and cultural destruction that denied the Dakota free and unhindered access to the land that fundamentally shapes their identity. We acknowledge that trauma has occurred, that harm continues to occur today, and that it is incumbent upon all of us residing on this land to work toward an equitable future where everyone has the opportunity to thrive. We encourage you, too, to learn and consider the history of the land on which you reside, as well as the resilient peoples and complex legacies that have made it what it is today.